'You're leaving?' Pierce was half on the veranda, half on the threshold as she walked past him.

'I need to.' Before she made a complete fool of herself and begged him not to listen to a word she was saying.

'Stacey—wait.'

She unlocked her car and put her bag inside before turning to face him, the driver's door between them.

'What about us? Isn't what we feel for each other worth pursuing?'

She reached out and placed a hand to his cheek, determined she wouldn't cry. 'If you love someone, set them free.' She smiled lovingly at the man who had stolen her heart, now and for evermore. 'You are going to be amazing. You are going to achieve such great things, and those great things are going to help so many people. I could never stand in the way of that.'

Her voice broke, and before she completely lost her resolve to set him free she turned from him, climbed into the car, shut the door and started the engine.

'Stacey!'

She tried not to hear the pleading in his tone as she carefully reversed out of the driveway, belatedly remembering to switch on her headlights. Even though they lived only a few blocks from each other she still had to pull over to wipe her tear-filled eyes because she couldn't see properly.

After she'd reached her house she headed quietly for her bedroom and, uncaring that she hadn't changed or brushed her teeth, lay down on her bed and allowed the tears to fall. She loved him. She loved Pierce with all her heart. But she could never live with herself if he sacrificed his own dreams for her. His dreams were his and he deserved the chance to achieve them.

'If you love someone, set them free. If they come back to you, they're yours. If they don't, they never were.' She recited the words into her pillow, hoping against hope that one day Pierce would return to her—because she would always be waiting for him.

Dear Reader

I've always loved reading linked stories—really getting to know characters and their family and friends—and now, with Stacey Wilton stepping out and leading the way, the Wilton triplets are making their mark. Stacey, Cora and Molly are three very different women, but they're joined in the bonds of sisterly love.

For ever the down-to-earth, sensible sister, Stacey thinks she's lost her chance at love—until she meets handsome Pierce Brolin. Such a gorgeous but determined man... I loved Pierce from the start. I love the way that he, like Stacey, who is guardian to her younger siblings, has such a strong grasp on the importance of family, on not taking the people he truly cares about for granted. It's inevitable that when these two meet they'll have an instant connection which will help them embrace all the various siblings—and rabbits—that weave their way throughout the story.

If there's one thing I've learned from the very important research required to write this story, it's that you're never too old to go on a swing!

Warmest regards

Lucy

DR PERFECT
ON HER DOORSTEP

BY
LUCY CLARK

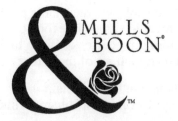

Lucy Clark is actually a husband-and-wife writing team. They enjoy taking holidays with their children, during which they discuss and develop new ideas for their books using the fantastic Australian scenery. They use their daily walks to talk over characterisation and fine details of the wonderful stories they produce, and are avid movie buffs. They live on the edge of a popular wine district in South Australia with their two children, and enjoy spending family time together at weekends.

Recent titles by Lucy Clark:

HER MISTLETOE WISH
THE SECRET BETWEEN THEM
RESISTING THE NEW DOC IN TOWN
ONE LIFE-CHANGING MOMENT
DARE SHE DREAM OF FOREVER?
FALLING FOR DR FEARLESS
DIAMOND RING FOR THE ICE QUEEN
TAMING THE LONE DOC'S HEART
THE BOSS SHE CAN'T RESIST
WEDDING ON THE BABY WARD
SPECIAL CARE BABY MIRACLE
DOCTOR DIAMOND IN THE ROUGH

**Praise for
Lucy Clark:**

'A sweet and fun romance
about second chances and second love.'
—*HarlequinJunkie* on
DARE SHE DREAM OF FOREVER?

CHAPTER ONE

STACEY WILTON PULLED the car to the side of the road. She looked across at the house, nostalgia rising within her. Turning the key to cut the engine, she unbuckled her seatbelt and opened the door, her gaze never leaving the house. The late-afternoon rays from the sun combined with the blue of the September sky only enhanced the beauty of the place.

It looked so different—smaller, somehow. Which was ridiculous, because houses didn't grow or shrink. And yet it was still the same as her memory recalled. The front garden had been re-landscaped, the large tree she and her sisters had used to climb was gone, and no shade fell over the front windows, but instead the garden was alive with rows of vibrantly coloured flowers, enjoying the spring weather. Stacey smiled. Her father would have loved that.

She leaned against the car and drank her fill of

the place she'd called home for the first fourteen years of her life. It was a place she'd never contemplated leaving, but she'd soon learned that life was never smooth. Her mother had walked out, abandoning them all.

Stacey and her sisters had been almost five years old, excited to start school, when their mother had declared that she'd had enough. Their father had been the local GP, working long and erratic hours. He'd employed a young nanny—Letisha—who, many years later, he'd married.

When he'd been head-hunted to run a new palliative care hospice in Perth Arn Wilton had accepted the position without consulting his teenage daughters.

'Why do we need to go?' Stacey had asked him, tears streaming down her face as he'd packed yet another box.

'Because this job is too good to pass up, Stace. I get to be a part of something new and exciting as well as incredibly important. This is the first palliative hospice just for children.'

'But what about all your patients *here*? What about your practice? I was going to become a doctor and then one day work with you here.'

'Stace.' Arn had sighed with resignation and placed a hand on her shoulder. 'It's time to move on.'

'Just because of a job? It doesn't make sense, Dad.'

'Well, then, think of Letisha. You love Letisha, and now that we're newly married it's not really fair to ask her to start her married life in a home where there have been so many unhappy memories. Tish deserves better, don't you think?'

When Stacey had opened her mouth to continue arguing her father had given her a stern look, which had meant the discussion was over.

Stacey and her sisters had packed their lives into boxes, said tearful goodbyes to their school friends, and hugged their neighbours, Edna and Mike, with tear-stained faces.

'I've never lived next door to anyone else,' Stacey had told Edna, who had been like a second mother to her.

'Adventures are good,' Edna had told her. 'And we'll keep in touch. I've given you enough letter paper and stamps to last you for a good two years at least.' Edna had smiled at her. 'We'll see each other again, Stacey.'

'Promise?' Stacey had asked.

'Promise.'

Then the Wilton family had left Newcastle, on Australia's east coast, and headed to Perth on the other side of the country. There they'd settled into their new life, and many years later Letisha had given birth to Stacey's new sister. Indeed, over the years their family had grown from three to six children.

Now, finally, after almost two decades, Stacey was returning to the job she'd always dreamed of: taking over the old family medical practice her father had once run. She hoped it would provide stability for all of them—especially after the events of the past eighteen months. Her father and beloved stepmother had passed away in a terrible car accident, leaving Stacey and her sisters as guardians of their younger siblings. Not only that, but Stacey had been jilted at the altar by the man who'd been supposed to love her for the rest of her life.

No, the past eighteen months had been soul-destroying, and her coming back to a town she'd always regarded as a place of solace was much needed.

'Can I help you?'

Stacey was pulled from her reverie by a man standing just at the edge of the driveway next to the house she was staring at. He was very tall, about six foot four, and wore an old pair of gardening shorts and a light blue T-shirt which he'd clearly used as a painting smock, if the splatters of green, yellow and pink paint were anything to go by. He had flip-flops on his feet, a peaked cap on his head, and a pair of gardening gloves on his hands. A pile of weeds was on the concrete driveway near his feet. How had she not seen him there before?

'Can I help you with something?' he repeated, taking off his gloves and tossing them carelessly onto the pile of weeds.

Stacey shifted her car keys from one hand to the other. 'No, thanks.'

'Are you sure? You seem to be quite entranced, just looking at my house.' He angled his head to the side, giving her a more concentrated look. 'Are you sure you're feeling all right?'

She waved away his concern and smiled politely. 'I'm fine… It's just that—well I used to live here.' She pointed to the house. 'When I was little.' She called her words across the street, feeling a little self-conscious as one or two cars drove between their impromptu conversation. When the man beckoned her over it seemed like the most logical thing in the world to cross the road and go and chat with a complete stranger.

'You've cut down the tree,' she said, pointing to where the tree used to be.

'Had to. It was diseased.'

'Oh. How sad. I guess it has been a while, but I do have such happy memories of climbing it—and swinging on the tyre swing.' Her sigh was nostalgic as she continued to peruse the garden. 'I really like the flowers. Very pretty.'

'Thank you. I don't mind doing a spot of gardening. I find it relaxing.'

'And painting? The house used to be a cream colour, but I think the mint-green looks much better. Good choice.'

The man nodded. 'I found painting very...therapeutic. I'd never painted a house before, but now I have. Both inside and out. One more thing crossed off my bucket list.'

Stacey gave him a puzzled look. 'Bucket what?'

'Bucket list. You know—a list of things you'd like to do before you pass away.'

She shook her head. 'I've never heard it put like that before. A bit morbid, isn't it?'

The man grinned—a full-on gorgeous smile that highlighted his twinkling blue eyes. Bedroom eyes, her sister Molly would have called them. Eyes that could mesmerise a woman from across the room...or across the road.

'Not morbid,' he continued, shaking his head a little. 'Adventurous. For example, if you had on your bucket list, *Talk to a strange man about bucket lists* then you could go home and cross that right off, feeling like you've actually accomplished something new today.'

Stacey's brow creased further. 'Why would I have that on a list of things I'd like to accomplish before I die?'

The man surprised her further by laughing. Was he laughing *at* her? Or at this bucket list thing he kept gabbing about?

'Never mind.' He held out his hand. 'I'm Pierce.'

She put her hand into his, ignoring the way the heat from this hand seemed to travel up her arm and explode into a thousand stars, setting her body alight.

'Stacey.' If she was the type of person to believe in instant attraction then she might be flattered by his smile. Thankfully she left that sort of emotion and nonsense up to Molly.

'Nice to meet you, Stacey.' Pierce gestured towards the house. 'Would you like to come inside? Take a look at some of the other changes we've made?'

We? He was most likely married, and as this house was perfect for children no doubt he had a couple of those as well. He seemed honest, personable and quite kind, but first impressions could be deceptive. Perhaps she should ask him some more questions, just to be sure.

She knew the Edelsteins still lived next door, as Edna had called her earlier that morning asking her to make a house call to review Mike.

'He's too stubborn to come to the clinic,' Edna had told her. 'But he'll listen to you, Stace.'

That was how Stacey found herself here, coming to see Mike and Edna. But now she was being invited by a stranger into the house where she'd grown up. Still, she should test the waters before going inside with him. Better to be safe than sorry.

'Do the Edelsteins still live next door?'

He nodded. 'That Edna… She's a talker, isn't she? Yesterday she stood at her fence for a good two hours and chatted to me while I did some gardening. I kept asking if she'd like to come and sit down on the veranda on the swing and have a nice cool drink—but, no, she was quite happy leaning on the fence and telling me all about her gallstone removal.'

Stacey smiled and nodded, pleased with the way Pierce's words held no impatience as he spoke of Edna. 'Same old Edna. And Mike? How's he doing?'

A frown furrowed his brow. 'Not too good, I'm sorry to say. I popped over last night just to check on him after Edna told me he's been getting increasingly dizzy when he stands up. Plus his asthma has flared, due to all the pollen.' Pierce pulled on his gardening gloves as he spoke and started tidying up the mound of weeds, placing them into the gardening recycle bin. 'His asthma meds are only just keeping things at bay.' He shook his head, concern evident in his tone.

Stacey nodded. This information was marrying up with what Edna had told her.

'Of course in typical fashion Mike's refusing to admit there's anything really wrong with him, but if things aren't brought under control soon he runs the risk of contracting pneumonia.'

'You sound very concerned.' Again she watched his expression, and when he met her eyes his gaze was quizzical.

'Of course I'm concerned. That's why I offered to give him a private check-up.'

Stacey's eyebrows hit her perfectly straight fringe. 'You're a doctor?'

Pierce nodded. 'GP. I've been doing locum work at the local hospital in the A & E department—just a few shifts a week while I finish getting things sorted out around here.'

A *doctor*? Her level of trust for Pierce increased. He was a doctor as well as passing her test regarding his neighbours. 'Well, thank you for checking up on Mike. What was your clinical assessment?'

'Clinical assessment, eh?' Pierce pondered her

words as he removed his gardening gloves and then snapped his fingers. 'That's *right*. Edna said a doctor used to live in this house and that some of his kids were also doctors.'

'That would have been my dad—Arn Wilton.'

'She said he was the only one who could ever make Mike see sense about health matters.'

Stacey's smile was nostalgic. 'He and Mike were always good friends.'

'Were? Did they have a falling out?'

'No. Not those two. Mates until the last.' Stacey looked down at the ground. 'My father and stepmother passed away eighteen months ago.'

'I'm sorry to hear that, Stacey.'

Pierce's tone was filled with compassion as well as understanding. She met his gaze once more and shrugged, annoyed with the tears that instantly sprang to her eyes. She blinked them away, wondering why she was telling this stranger so much about her life. It had to be this house—the memories it brought back.

'Losing parents is never easy. Mine both passed away almost a decade ago and still there are days when I miss them a lot.' He exhaled slowly, then shrugged one shoulder. 'I have questions. Ones only they would know how to answer.'

'Yes.' The word was heartfelt, as though somehow the loss of parents and the pain it caused had formed a bond between the two of them. 'Instead it leaves us floundering around, trying to figure things out on our own.'

He nodded, but didn't stop looking intently at her, and for some reason Stacey found it nigh impossible to look away. Pierce seemed to be a decent and caring man—a family man content to care for his home as well as his neighbours. She had no idea why he was only working as a locum at the local hospital, but presumably he had his reasons for not wanting to take on a more permanent position. Perhaps he wanted to spend some time working his way through his bucket list.

She paused as a different thought occurred to her. Perhaps he had a terminal illness, or was recovering from one. He didn't look gaunt. In fact he looked positively healthy. Stacey stopped her thoughts. This man was not her patient. He was not a puzzle for her to solve, to figure out what was wrong with him and then try to find a solution. But it was such an integrated part of her personality—especially being the oldest sibling in her family.

'By five minutes.'

She instantly heard her sister Cora's protest, which came every time Stacey stated that fact. Nevertheless, five minutes was five minutes, and Stacey took her responsibilities seriously.

'Anyway…' Pierce was first to break the silence as he put the lid down on the green recycle bin. 'I didn't mean to take our conversation in such a maudlin direction. You asked about Mike. Chest is extremely tight, asthma meds are providing basic relief, but I think the chest pains might be worse than he's letting on. Edna said he'd been dizzy, but I didn't take my otoscope with me and when I suggested he see someone about it, to make sure it wasn't the start of something a bit more sinister, he growled at me and kicked me out of his house.'

'He always did have a good bark.' Stacey's smile was instant as she followed Pierce towards the house, quietly amazed at how comfortable she was around him. 'Edna asked me to pop over once I'd finished clinic.'

'That's why you're here? To give Mike a check-up?'

'Yes, but I can see Edna's car's not in the driveway, so I'll wait until she gets home.'

'And your question about neighbours was a test, eh?' He grinned, crossing his arms over his broad chest. 'I take it I passed?'

'Yes.'

'Excellent.' He jerked his thumb towards the house. 'Does this mean you feel safe enough to come and take a look around inside?'

Stacey nodded, excitement starting to build. She told herself it was because she was getting the chance to see inside the house, rather than because she was getting to spend a bit more time with the handsome Dr Pierce.

'Where are you working?' Pierce asked conversationally as they crossed the veranda and entered the house.

'I've recently bought my father's old GP practice.'

'The one up the road? Shortfield Family Medical Practice?'

'That's the one. Phillip Morcombe took over the practice from my father sixteen years ago, and when I realised it was up for sale—' Stacey stopped as she stood on the other side of the threshold, her gaze drinking in the living room of the house which held all her earliest memories.

'Oh!' She clutched her hands to her chest. 'That's where my sisters and I used to lie on our stomachs after school and watch half an hour of television.' She pointed to the middle of the room. 'And the bay window. There used to be a curtain that separated it off from the rest of the room and that used to be our secret corner, where we'd spend hours whispering our best secrets to each other. Or we'd curl up with a book and just read.' She smiled. 'Well, Cora and I read books. Molly could never sit still. Still can't.'

'How old are your sisters? You sound so close.'

'You don't know the half of it,' Stacey said with a grin. 'We're triplets. Non-identical,' she added, as a matter of routine. She waited, expecting the usual reaction of, *Wow. Triplets? I've never met triplets before,* or *Can you sense each other's emotions?* or *How far apart are the three of you? Who's the eldest?* but all Pierce did was smile widely.

'What a lot of fun you must have had.' His tone sounded almost wistful. 'So close, so connected.'

Stacey mulled over his words as he headed around to the kitchen and dining room. 'Are you an only child?'

'I was. For quite a while. I was fifteen when my sister was born. She was born very late in my parents' life, but they loved each and every moment they had with Nell.'

He walked into the kitchen and pointed to a framed photograph up on the wall—one of him and a lovely-looking young woman who was staring at him with open delight, as though he'd just handed her the moon.

'That was taken six months ago, at Nell's twenty-first birthday. I'd just given her the keys to this house. Independent living.' There was a thrill of pride in his tone as he looked at the picture of his sister.

Stacey processed his words. 'You've done all this work with the house for your *sister*?'

'It's been Nell's goal. She's been working towards it for so long and we're almost ready…in about another three months' time.'

'You're not married?' Why had that question

sounded as though she was fishing for information? 'Er… I… You don't have to answer that.
It's really none of my business.'

'Married? Me?' Pierce shook his head emphat-
ically. 'No. *No.* No, no, no, no, no.'

'So that's a no?' she remarked drolly, wondering if his determined answer hinted at matri-
monial issues. She tried not to frown, tried not
to lump him into the same category as another
specific male she knew who had also had deeply
rooted issues with marriage and commitment.

'I'd do anything for Nell.' As he said the words
he quickly checked his watch, then gasped. 'And
that includes going to meet her at the bus stop.
Come on, Stacey.' Pierce grabbed her hand and
tugged her back through the house, across the
veranda and into the garden. 'We're going to be
late.'

'We?' She pulled her hand free. 'Er… I'll leave
you to it.'

'But you have *got* to meet Nell. She'd love to
meet someone who used to live here. She adores
this house. She picked it out five years ago and
told me that was the house she was going to live

in when she was twenty-one. She's very stubborn and adamant, my sister.'

'Well, then, I'll go next door and see if Edna's home yet and—'

'There's no time for discussion now.'

Pierce grabbed her hand again and started tugging her along with him as he quickened his pace, pointing in the distance to a bus that was drawing closer.

'That's her bus! We've got to make it to the bus stop in time. Usually she can cope if I'm not there to greet her, but her whole routine has been a little out of whack lately—what with her promotion at work and all the new things she's had to learn. Hence me meeting her bus is the one absolute she needs in her life right now.'

Pierce spouted this information quickly as they continued towards the bus stop. When he broke into a jog as the bus drew closer Stacey had no option but to go along with him. As they jogged she had to confess she was rather intrigued at the way Pierce spoke about his sister.

They arrived at the bus stop just as the young woman from the photograph was climbing down the back steps of the bus, stepping onto the pavement. She looked around, anxiety etched on her features, but the instant she saw Pierce running towards her, the anxiety cleared and a wide, beaming smile brightened her face.

'I got scared. I could not see you, Pierce. But now you are here.' Nell, who had shoulder-length blonde hair and blue eyes that matched her brother's, spoke every word perfectly, but with little inflection.

Pierce let go of Stacey's hand before enveloping his sister in a hug. 'Sorry, Nellie. I was gardening and forgot the time.'

He took Nell's bag from her and slipped his arm around her waist as Nell started off down the street, counting her steps. She didn't seem to notice Stacey at all, and as Pierce beckoned for her to follow them, Stacey's sharp medical mind began sifting through the information she knew.

Nell had been born to a more mature mother, and clearly needed a strict routine. She hadn't paid any attention to Stacey, even though Stacey had been holding hands with Pierce. The fact that Pierce hadn't tried to introduce Stacey, instead allowing his sister to continue counting the steps from the bus stop to the house, alerted her to the fact that while Nell might appear to be a beautiful young twenty-one-year-old on the outside, mentally her age was far younger.

It wasn't until they were standing on the front veranda of the house that Nell stopped counting and turned to smile at her brother. 'I got it right. The same number as yesterday.'

'That's great, Nellie.' He removed his arm from his sister's waist and turned to indicate Stacey. 'There's someone I want you to meet.' It was only then that Nell seemed to notice Stacey's presence. 'Nell, this is Stacey.'

Dutifully, Nell held out her hand to Stacey and shook it firmly. 'Hello, Stacey. I am very pleased to meet you.' She nodded and smiled, as though she was secretly proud of herself for getting the greeting correct.

'Good girl,' Pierce said softly. Nell let go of Stacey's hand, her smile increasing at her brother's praise. 'I know this is your house now, Nell, but when Stacey was a little girl she and her sisters used to live here.'

Nell looked from Stacey to Pierce and back again, as though slowly processing the words. 'Really?' Her eyes widened with delight. 'Did you sleep in the same room as me? The pink room?'

Stacey smiled and nodded. 'The room was definitely pink.'

'Why don't you show Stacey your room now?' Pierce encouraged as he opened the door, holding it for the women to precede him.

'Yes!' Nell entered the house and clutched her hands to her chest with the excitement of a child at Christmas. 'I *love* my room. Did you love it, too, when it was your room?'

'Yes. I really did.' Allowing Nell's excitement to affect her, Stacey followed the young woman down the hallway.

Nell was delighted to show Stacey her doll collection, as well as a cupboard full of puzzles. Jigsaw puzzles, wooden puzzles, metal ones too.

'You must be very good at puzzles, Nell.'

'Yes. I am. My brother says that I have an amazing puzzle brain.'

She grinned, and Stacey couldn't help but instantly warm to her.

'He is so funny.'

'Afternoon snacks are ready,' Pierce called,

and Nell immediately turned and set off for the kitchen.

'I like afternoon snacks. Do *you* like afternoon snacks, Stacey?'

'I do, Nell.' Stacey smiled as she watched Nell politely thank her brother before sitting down at the kitchen bench to attend to her food. They all ate, Pierce having prepared fruit with cheese and a glass of juice for himself and Stacey as well.

'How was work, Nell?'

'It was good, Pierce.' Nell swallowed her mouthful.

'Nell works as a researcher for a computer company. She solves a lot of their internal programming issues.' Pierce offered the information for Stacey's benefit, but Nell nodded as though to confirm it.

'That sounds impressive,' Stacey added.

'It is.' Nell ate another mouthful.

'Did you do anything exciting today?'

Pierce continued with his questions and Stacey had the feeling it was all part of their routine.

'Yes. I solved the number puzzle Mr Jorgensen could not do. He said I did it really fast.' Nell preened a little, feeling good about herself. 'I like puzzles.'

Once Nell had finished eating she stacked her plate and glass in the dishwasher before announcing that it was time to watch television. Off she went, leaving Stacey sitting at the table with Pierce. He watched his sister in the other room, a proud smile playing about his lips, and when he looked back at Stacey he saw she was watching him intently.

'Higher functioning autism,' he stated as he drank the last of his drink.

'She's doing very well for herself,' Stacey remarked, finishing her juice.

Pierce nodded as he collected their glasses and stacked them in the dishwasher. 'She is, and I have to say I'm very proud of her.'

'So I can see.' Stacey grinned. 'And thank you for the snack. I can't remember the last time I actually sat and had an after-work snack.'

'It's Nell's routine.'

'What happens if you're at the hospital when she gets home from work?'

'I try to be here most days, but if I'm not at the bus stop to meet her then Edna or Mike usually help out. And if that's not possible, and I know I'm going to be delayed, I'll ring Nell and let her know before she gets off the bus. But thankfully those days are few and far between.'

'If you need further support I'd be happy to add Nell to our practice nurse visitation list.'

He nodded. 'I was going to suggest something like that. I'm so glad you've bought the practice. We all thought it was going to close completely.'

'I know. My father's old partner retired last year, and since then there have been various locums running it.'

'A practice can't survive like that. It definitely needs someone at the helm.'

Stacey spread her arms wide. 'As you see.'

'You're running it by yourself?'

'Uh…with my sisters. Well, sort of. We all own the practice equally and Winifred the practice nurse, who has been there for years, is staying on—thank goodness.'

'Ah, yes. We've met Winifred several times. She's lovely.' Pierce leaned back in his chair and watched her for a moment. 'I take it both your sisters are doctors, too?'

'Yes. We went through medical school together, did all our GP training together.'

'And what do you mean by "sort of"? Your sisters are "sort of" running the practice with you? How does that work?'

Stacey frowned as she thought about Molly's new plans to study surgery. She was proud and delighted with her sister's accomplishments, but it did put her in a bit of a bind.

'Actually, my sister Molly has decided to study surgery.'

He raised his eyebrows at this. 'She's been accepted to a surgical training programme?'

'Yes.'

'Here?'

'Yes, at Newcastle General. A place came up at the last minute so she took it. Effective immediately.'

He nodded. 'Good for her.'

Pierce leaned one elbow on the table and rested his head on his hand, giving her his undivided attention. She shifted in the seat but forced herself to remain calm and collected as she placed her hands in her lap.

He continued just to sit there, watching her

as though she were a complete mystery to him. When he raised a questioning eyebrow she spread her hands wide. 'What? Is there something on my nose? Do I have milk on my lip?'

Pierce smiled and shook his head. Good heavens! Did the man have *any* idea just how lethal that small, gorgeous smile of his could be? The way it caused the corners of his eyes to crinkle with delight? The way it made her feel as though he wasn't trying to judge her, just trying to understand her? For all intents and purposes this man was a stranger to her, and yet for some reason she felt so comfortable around him. It was an odd sensation, but with both Cora and Molly telling her to loosen up, to step outside her comfort zone, start living her life for *her* instead of everyone else, and with Pierce smiling at her so acceptingly, Stacey found herself telling him things she usually wouldn't tell anyone.

'Yes—yes, it *is* good for Molly. She's always wanted to do it. But it does leave me somewhat in the lurch. Cora, my other sister, is over in Tarparnii at the moment, working with Pacific Medical Aid.'

'An excellent organisation. I have…friends who do a lot of work with them.'

Stacey wondered at his hesitation. Were they his friends or weren't they? 'Are you interested in going to work there, too?'

He shrugged. 'Maybe. One day.'

'It's not on your bucket list?'

Pierce grinned. 'There are a lot of other things on my bucket list so I'll attend to them first.' He gestured to the house. 'And first on the list is to get this place completely shipshape for Nell and her soon-to-be housemates.'

'She has friends who are moving in, too?'

'Two other fine young ladies who she works with. Loris is in a wheelchair, which is why I need to finish getting all the ramps made, and Samantha has high-functioning Asperger's.'

'Sounds like it's important for me to get to know all of them.'

'Yes. Your medical practice will be the closest one for all of them. But where Nell is concerned, if she knows you on a more personal level then she's more likely to come to you when she needs help.'

'And we'll help in any way we can.' She smiled politely.

Pierce nodded with thanks, then looked at her thoughtfully. 'Hang on a minute. If Molly's studying surgery at the hospital, and Cora is overseas, then who *is* running the clinic with you?'

'Molly does a day here and there, and she's promised to find me a locum to cover for her.'

There was silence between them for a minute, with the clock on the mantel ticking loudly. Pierce continued to watch her intently, leaning his head on his hand. Stacey started to feel highly self-conscious as he just looked at her... stopped everything and *really* looked. What did he see?

'All right.' Pierce straightened up and slapped his hand onto the table, making her jump. 'I'll do it!'

'What? What will you do?' Stacey asked, startled by his abrupt behaviour.

'Call your sister. Tell her the search is over.'

'What search?' Stacey stared at him as though he'd grown an extra head.

'The locum search.' He stood and held out his hand to her. 'Dr Pierce Brolin, at your service.'

Stacey shook his hand, still a little dazed. 'I'm not sure I underst—'

'I'm coming to work for you. I'm your new locum.'

CHAPTER TWO

STACEY UNLOCKED THE front door of the family medical practice and headed to the light switch, illuminating the reception area and waiting room. It was early. Just after seven-thirty on a Monday morning. And although her first patient wasn't due to walk through the doors for another hour she'd been too nervous to sleep.

She sniffed. The air still smelled faintly of paint, and she quickly located the air filters she'd purchased last week and switched them on. If it wasn't for the rain outside she'd open the windows, but the September weather was giving them the runaround—one day sunny, the next pouring with rain.

Stacey walked through the practice, opening blinds and switching on the equipment that needed to be on. She refused to dwell on the second consulting room—the one which would be assigned to Pierce Brolin, whose first official day in the clinic would be starting in about an hour's time.

Had she done the right thing? It was true she needed a locum. It was true that Pierce was not only available but also extremely willing. His credentials were certainly impressive—especially his extensive experience in autism spectrum disorders—so she couldn't understand why he wasn't working in his chosen specialty.

'I'm more than happy to fill the gap while you wait for your sister Cora to return to Newcastle,' he'd told her when they'd met last week to sign the legal contracts.

It had been on the tip of her tongue to ask him *why* he was happy to help out here and there, but it really was none of her business. Perhaps he was content to get things settled for Nell without having the stress of a full-time workload hanging over his head. All that mattered was that Pierce was a qualified doctor who was willing to help her out.

She had to leave it at that, had to keep her emotional distance from him, because he was definitely an enigmatic man who was able to make her feel as though she were the most important person in the world. The way he smiled at her, the way he shook her hand, the way he gave her his undivided attention when he talked... All of those little things were things that Robert had never done.

She closed her eyes as an image of Robert's stern face came to mind. Her ex-fiancé, although professing to love and care about her, had never really shown it. She'd always rationalised it— Robert wasn't the demonstrative type—but now that she'd had quite a bit of time to reflect on her failed relationship she'd come to realise that he simply hadn't loved her as much as he'd said.

He'd never held her hand in public, never leaned over and whispered something intimate in her ear, never looked at her across a crowded room as though he wanted everyone to instantly disappear just so he could be alone with her.

When she'd been sitting at her consulting room desk, with Pierce on the other side, carefully reading the locum contract, Molly and Winifred both hovering around and chatting, Stacey had been far too aware of him. His broad shoulders, his thoughtful brow, his twinkling blue eyes when he'd lifted his head and looked at her, somehow making her feel as though he could see right into her soul…

And that had been the moment. That one true moment in time when nothing else seemed to matter. Her mouth had instantly gone dry, the other people in the room had disappeared from her view and it had been just the two of them, Pierce had stared into her eyes and she'd stared back into his. Neither of them had moved, and she could have sworn that the spinning of the earth had actually slowed down, capturing them both in a bubble of time. It had been an odd sensation, but for that one split second Stacey had felt…*accepted*. Without reservation, without condition.

She shook her head, clearing it of the image. 'And he'll be working here,' she murmured as she made herself walk into the consulting room he'd been assigned.

Even now she could picture him sitting behind the desk, looking up at her as she came in to speak to him about something, their eyes meeting and holding once more. Did she yearn for that sensation again because he'd made her feel accepted? Or did she fear the sensation because he'd so easily been able to penetrate the fortress she'd worked hard to put in place after Robert had broken her heart?

She glanced around the room, opening one or two of the cupboards to ensure they were properly stocked with everything he might need. She wanted today to go well, for Pierce to be happy working here.

After she'd left his home over two weeks ago Stacey hadn't been sure which way to turn. She'd known basically nothing about the man, and yet there he'd been, offering his services to help her out. Was he just being kind or was he a bit loopy?

All she could remember doing at the time was murmuring a polite reply to his declaration that he was going to work with her and then excusing herself. Her thoughts had been in such a jumble that she'd almost forgotten to check on Mike Edelstein—which had been the main reason for her being in that part of town. She'd walked out to her car to retrieve her medical bag, and been surprised to find Pierce waiting by the Edelsteins' front door by the time she reached it.

'We may as well review him together,' he'd stated, before knocking on the door.

Stacey had barely had time to collect her thoughts before Edna had opened the door and welcomed them both inside.

The other woman had hugged Stacey close. 'It's good to see you again, love,' Edna had said as she'd embraced Stacey. 'Although I wish it was in better circumstances. But at least now that you're here we might finally get Mike to see some sense, eh? He always had time for you, Stace.'

Mike had indeed been happy to see her, but when Stacey had insisted upon giving him a check-up he'd fussed about, telling her she was blowing the entire thing out of proportion.

He stabbed a finger at Pierce. 'If this young whipper-snapper hadn't been hanging around the side fence the other day he never would have heard me coughing.' Mike glared at Edna. 'At least that's what he *said*. But chances are Edna dragged him inside because she was stressing over nothing.'

'Mike—' Stacey began, but Mike was in full swing, his words peppered by coughs.

'Came right over, he did. Sticking his nose in where it doesn't belong, telling me I had problems with my lungs. Well, of course I do. I've had asthma for most of me life, and I know when it's bad and when it's good and right now it's fine. Just fine, I tell you.'

But the instant Mike finished protesting his body was racked with a coughing spasm.

Stacey instantly rubbed Mike's back, encouraging him quietly to relax and breathe slowly. Her soothing tone must have done something, because Mike's bluster seemed to disappear.

'There's one thing I want to remind you of,' she said as she placed her medical bag beside his comfortable lounge chair.

'Yeah? What's that?' he asked, lifting his chin and meeting her gaze, pure stubbornness reflected in his eyes.

'You may be stubborn, but I'm my father's daughter—which therefore means that my stubbornness trumps yours every time.'

Edna laughed. 'She's got you there, Mikey.' And then, as though everything was now right with her world, Edna declared that she'd go and put the kettle on.

With resigned reluctance, Mike agreed to the check-up.

'Pierce was right,' Stacey said as she packed away her stethoscope and closed her medical bag once her review was complete. 'Your asthma is very bad and your ears are red. Your throat's not the best, either. You'll need some antibiotics, and I want you up at the hospital first thing tomorrow for a chest X-ray to check you're not on the way to contracting pneumonia. Spring is notorious for ailments such as chest infections, and right now it's the last thing you need—what with the rabbit jumping season quickly approaching.'

'Oh, we don't compete any more,' Edna said in a loud whisper as she carried in a tray of tea and biscuits. 'Our ol' Vashta passed away a few years ago. What a champion that rabbit was.' Edna sighed and looked wistful for a moment, before shaking her head once more.

'But you still go to watch, don't you?' Stacey asked, 'I was telling the children about it just last night and all of them were eager to go. Lydia was even asking if we could get a rabbit ourselves. She adores them.'

'Really?' Light shone in Edna's eyes as she'd

placed the tray on the table and stood next to Stacey.

'I was also hoping that if I was stuck at the clinic, or if Molly was in surgery, you two might be able to take the children to the rabbit jumping show for me?' Stacey's tone held a hint of pleading, and as she watched them closely, knowing Mike had always loved to help others, especially when it concerned his favourite animals, she saw a flicker of light come back into his old eyes.

'Lydia's interested, eh? How old is she now?'

'She's seven—and just as stubborn as me.'

'Hmm…' Mike stroked his chin with thumb and forefinger. 'Seven, you say? Seven's just about the right age to start.'

Edna reached out and held Stacey's hand as they both watched Mike closely. He contemplated this information seriously for a moment or two before nodding.

'OK, then. I'll go to the hospital and take the antibiotics and do whatever else it is you want me to do—but only because it's important that I'm there to instruct little Lydia right from the beginning. There are many responsibilities that go hand in hand with wanting to raise a champion jumper. This isn't a normal pet we're talking about. She has to be one hundred per cent committed to the entire process.'

'Excellent. I'll inform Lydia when I get home tonight. She'll be ecstatic. But...' Stacey levelled Mike with her best no-nonsense look '...you must do everything I, or Pierce, or any other doctor who treats you prescribes. Deal?' She held out her hand, never once breaking eye contact with Mike.

Mike sat up a little straighter in his chair and held her gaze before he reached out and shook hands with Stacey.

'Deal.'

Edna squealed with delight and clapped her hands. 'Mike agreeing to treatment *and* the chance to pass on our love of rabbit jumping to the next generation!' She kissed Mike's cheek and then gave Stacey a big hug.

Stacey smiled before packing up her equipment into the medical bag and handing the prescription for antibiotics to Edna.

'Well played,' Pierce whispered close by.

Stacey hadn't realised he was standing so close. She looked at him over her shoulder.

'Gotta have a few tricks up your sleeve when it comes to persuading Mike to do something.'

'So I see.'

He accepted the cup of tea Edna offered him, as did Stacey. Mike started to breathe more easily, thanks to the medication Stacey had given him. He relaxed back in his chair, a smile on his face, as he regaled them with anecdotes about his beloved sport of rabbit jumping and exactly what he'd need to teach Lydia.

By the time they left Mike was settled and Edna was happy.

'It's good to see that you have an excellent bedside manner,' Pierce said as he walked her across the road to her car.

Stacey unlocked it and stowed her medical bag in the back seat. 'Thank you.'

'I'm going to enjoy working alongside you, Dr Stacey.'

And then he'd taken her hand in his, gently shaking it, and the action had been more slow and intentional than in a normal brisk business handshake.

'*Very* much.'

Stacey closed her eyes and rubbed her hands

together, the memory of that hand-shake, the memory of his deep, sensual tone, still managing to make her tremble. What was it about him that seemed to tilt her world off its axis? When she thought about Pierce she had the oddest sensation of excitement, of anticipatory delight. But she'd had those sensations once before, with Robert, and look how *that* had turned out.

Opening her eyes, she turned away from Pierce's consulting room, forcing herself to stop thinking about the way it had felt to have her hand wrapped securely in his, or the way his eyes had seemed to be able see right into the depths of her soul. He was just another doctor who was helping her out. Nothing more. The slight buzz of awareness she felt whenever she was around him was simply because she was grateful.

There was no need for her to try and figure him out, to understand why he was content to work in part-time jobs, helping out here and there in a medical capacity. The fact of the matter was that his help was needed and she'd accepted it for the next three months until Cora's return.

Where or what Pierce Brolin did after that was nothing to do with her.

She headed to the kitchen and turned on the coffee machine, checking there was sufficient milk in the fridge to get them through the rest of the day. 'Business,' she told herself sternly. 'It's all just business.'

'Knock, knock.'

Stacey gasped at the sound of the deep male voice, spinning around so fast she bumped her hip against the fridge door.

'Pierce!' She rubbed at her hip.

'Are you OK? Sorry. Didn't mean to startle you. I thought you would have heard the bell as I opened the front door.' He twirled a small key chain around his finger before putting the keys into his trouser pocket.

'I was…thinking.' *About you*, she added silently, and quickly turned away, busying herself with making coffee.

'So I heard. It's all just business, right?'

Stacey closed her eyes for a second, unable to believe he'd heard her talking to herself but glad that at this moment he couldn't see her face. 'Something like that.' She needed to change the subject. 'Can I get you a drink?' She turned to face him. 'Tea? Coffee?'

'No, I'm fine.' He pulled out a chair and sat down at the small kitchen table. 'Thought I'd get in early and go over my patient notes for the day.'

'Fair enough.'

'How about you? Couldn't sleep?'

She frowned for a moment, knowing she could never tell him that she'd awoken around five-thirty that morning from a dream in which he'd been caressing her cheek, his gaze intent on hers, seeing into her soul once more and making her feel more alive than she'd ever felt before.

'Er…busy thoughts.' Well, that was sort of true.

'Aha. Anything to do with rabbit jumping?'

When she angled her head to the side in slight confusion, he elaborated.

'I was talking to Mike last night—who, I must say, is doing much better. Anyway, he mentioned that you've recently bought two potential champion rabbits.'

Stacey forced herself to relax and nodded. The rabbits. A very safe topic. 'Yes. Lydia and George insisted on having one rabbit each.'

'How old is George?'

'Nine. He said if Lydia was old enough to get a rabbit then he was doubly old enough because he was two years older.'

Pierce watched as she moved around the kitchen, making herself a cup of coffee. How was it she could perform the simplest of tasks with such grace? All her movements were fluid and seamless, and he was entranced. In fact ever since he'd met Stacey Wilton he'd been intrigued. Bit by bit he was discovering more about her, and each new piece of the puzzle was unique as well as confusing.

George? Who was George? He'd presumed that the seven-year-old Lydia she'd mentioned was her daughter. Did Stacey also have a nine-year-old son? If so, where was the father of these children? She didn't wear a wedding ring, and there had been no mention of a husband. He tried to remember whether Mike or Edna had said anything, but Mike had been far more interested in discussing the rabbits rather than the children.

'Sounds fair.' He kept his tone at a neutral level whilst his mind tried to compute any new information he might uncover. 'I know Nell's very interested, but I don't think we'll be buying a rabbit any time soon.'

'She's more than welcome to help Lydia and George if she likes. We only live two blocks away from you, so our houses are within easy walking distance.'

'Thank you, Stacey.' He seemed genuinely surprised by the offer. 'That's nice of you.'

She pulled out a chair and sat at the opposite end of the table to him. 'Having Nell come round might actually prove a worthwhile diversion for Jasmine.'

'Jasmine?'

'She's just turned fourteen, so at the moment she's nothing but hormones.' Stacey slumped forward a little and sighed.

A fourteen-year-old as well! Stacey must have been a young mother. Either that or she was older than he'd initially thought. He managed to hide his surprise. 'Ah. I remember that phase with Nell—which, believe me, wasn't easy. Trying to explain hormones and why she would feel such extremes in her emotions was difficult, especially as our parents had passed away only a few years before. But we figured it all out in the end.'

Stacey sipped her drink. 'That helps put things with Jasmine into perspective. The teenage years are the worst, in my opinion. But of course Jasmine doesn't think I understand. She's still mad at me for dragging her away from all her friends in Perth, three-quarters of the way through the school year, to the other side of the country.'

'I guess it's not easy for you—especially without your parents around.'

'No.' She sat up a little straighter and stared down into her coffee cup. 'Cora keeps telling me that Jasmine will settle down, and Molly's really good with her, but she blames me for everything at the moment, whether it's my fault or not.'

'It's just a phase, Stacey. She'll grow out of it.'

'Let's hope she does that before I lose complete and utter patience with her.'

Pierce chuckled. 'Where are the kids now?'

Stacey checked the clock on the wall. 'Probably finishing off their breakfast and getting ready for school.'

'How do they get to school?' Did she have a nanny?

'Molly's on a late shift. She and I usually co-ordinate if we can, but now that Jasmine's a little older she's responsible for getting George and Lydia to school each morning.'

'Jasmine won't be tempted to cut class if there's no one to check up on her?'

'Oh, gosh. I hadn't even thought of that.' She stared at him for a moment, holding his gaze, the despair slowly disappearing from her face.

Did the woman have any idea just how beautiful she was? Especially when she looked at him like that, all vulnerable and soft. Right at this moment in time he didn't really care how many children she had, or what sort of shenanigans she might be facing at home. All he was aware of was how lovely Stacey Wilton was. She was the reason why he'd been unable to sleep that morning, with his thoughts turning to what it might be like to work alongside her, to see her on a regular basis, and whether or not something else might be brewing between them.

Then she blinked, and with an abruptness that startled him she stood and finished her coffee before taking the cup to the sink and washing it.

'At any rate, I'd best go and review my own

set of patients before the busy day begins,' she mumbled.

And within another moment, Pierce found himself alone in the small kitchen.

'Uh...' She poked her head around the door. 'Just let me know if you need help with anything. And er...welcome to Shortfield Family Medical Practice.' She didn't quite meet his gaze as she spoke, and as soon as she'd finished her little spiel she headed off once more.

Pierce exhaled slowly and pushed both hands through his hair. Stacey Wilton was a whirlwind of a woman—buying her own medical practice, moving her family across country, juggling a full-time job and three children. She was dynamic, thoughtful...and incredibly sexy.

He hadn't wanted to think of her in such a way, especially as they would be working together for the next few months, but he'd come to accept it as fact. The way she held herself, the way she walked with a slight swish of her hips, the way she occasionally tucked her shoulder-length brown hair behind her ear... Her eyes were the blue of the sky on a cloudless day, and her lips were... Well, whenever he thought about the shape of her mouth his gut would tighten, because the urge to actually see what those lips tasted like was a thought he hadn't been able to dismiss at all.

It wasn't as if he lusted after every new woman he met—in fact quite the opposite. After Catherine had ended their engagement six years ago he'd tried to date, but as soon as they discovered he was his autistic sister's sole guardian most women would usually choose not to see him again. Catherine, of course, had been different. She'd been instantly loving and accepting of Nell. But even that had had its flaws.

He stood up quickly, almost knocking over his chair, determined to control his thoughts. There was no point in reflecting on the past—not now, when he was at the beginning of the next junction of his life. Just three more months. By then Nell would be completely settled at the house, along with her two housemates, and he could finally accept his dream job—the job he'd been offered several times already but had been forced to decline. Until Nell was ready there was no chance he'd ever be able to leave.

As things stood, he'd been putting his plans

into place for a long time, ensuring Nell under-stood as much as possible about what would be happening, teaching her how to talk on the in-ternet chat channel he'd set up and other things like that. He wasn't going to leave his sister in the lurch—she was as much a part of him as his arm or his leg—but the chance to finally com-plete his research, to work with other staff who shared his passion for understanding as much as possible about autism spectrum disorders, would be brilliant.

He'd already completed a lot of research, writ-ten and published several scientific papers on the positive and negative effects of independent living in the autistic adult, and he knew he'd figured out how to provide the right amount of independence and support for Nell—support which could be given via computer or phone. He was so close to achieving his goal, to finally being able to accept the position he'd been cov-eting for years. The last thing he needed was to form some sort of romantic attachment to a woman who was clearly devoted to her own family.

Stacey was lovely. There was no denying that.

But he still had no idea whether or not she was married. And so Stacey Wilton, for several reasons, was off-limits—even to his thoughts.

CHAPTER THREE

OVER THE NEXT week Stacey couldn't believe how easy she found life working alongside Pierce Brolin. It really was as though he'd been sent from heaven just when she needed him most. He was even still working two shifts per week at the hospital, determined to honour his commitments.

'Nell was asking to see you again,' Pierce mentioned on Thursday afternoon, after they'd finished a hectic clinic.

Stacey had ventured into his consulting room to see how he'd fared during the busy day, and when he offered her a chair she gratefully accepted.

'Oh, that's nice. How is she?' Stacey sat down, sighing with relief at finally being off her feet.

'More interested in meeting your rabbits than in seeing you, if I own the truth.' He grinned as he spoke and Stacey laughed, the lilting sound washing over him. He swallowed and ignored the effect. They were colleagues and friends. Nothing more. 'How about dinner this Saturday night?' Friends could have dinner.

Stacey thought for a moment. 'Are you sure you're prepared for all of us to come?'

'The whole gaggle,' he confirmed. 'I'd like to meet the children and the rabbits, and if your sister's free ask her to come along, too. The more the merrier.'

Stacey frowned for a moment. The children *and* her sister? Didn't he realise that they were one and the same? Well, apart from poor George, who was clearly not a sister.

'Nell won't be upset with having too many people in the house? We're a pretty rowdy bunch.'

'She's usually pretty good with people if she's been properly prepared. Plus it's good for her to stretch her boundaries. It's one of the reasons why she's desperate to live independently, and the more people she knows and can rely on the better it's going to be for her.'

'True. I've read your papers on the subject. Very interesting.' She tried not to colour as she spoke, not wanting to confess that she'd actually looked him up on the internet and discovered a link to his scientific papers. In fact he appeared quite the expert on the subject of adults with autism and their integration into society.

'Thanks.' He nodded once, acknowledging her praise, but quickly continued. 'So you'll all come?'

Stacey thought over his invitation. 'Well, I'll tentatively accept on behalf of us all, but if I can let you know definite numbers tomorrow that would be great.'

'Glad to see you don't rule the roost with an iron will.'

'No. We're very much a democracy—except when it comes to bedtime.' She shook her head and chuckled. 'George always has to push the limits.'

'That's what nine-year-old boys do, I'm afraid.' Pierce joined in with her laughter, his curiosity about Stacey and these children still highly piqued.

During the week he'd discovered that Stacey wasn't married, or involved with anyone, because he'd overheard one of their more senior patients asking her when she was going to settle down and get married.

Stacey's answer had been polite. 'Not just yet, Mrs Donahue.'

Even though he'd tried to ignore his naturally inquisitive nature, he hadn't been able to stop himself from trying to figure her out. While he respected her privacy, there was something about Stacey—something about the way she seemed to be so tightly wound, taking life very seriously. He knew from talking to Mike and Edna that Stacey and her two sisters had recently turned thirty-one. That was hardly old, and yet she seemed so much older in her mannerisms and in the way her life seemed to be so closely structured.

Perhaps that was the reason he was interested in getting to know her a bit more. Perhaps he'd unconsciously decided to help her to find life a bit more vibrant, a bit more happy during his time here. For the moment, though, he realised the conversation they'd been having had come to an end, and it would look silly if he just continued to sit in the chair opposite her and stare, as he was doing right now.

'OK, then. Saturday night around six o'clock—family approval and patients willing?'

He stood from the chair and came around the desk, aware that Stacey was watching his every move. He leaned on the desk and crossed his legs at the ankle, trying to ignore the way her light visual caress made him want to preen.

'Uh…sure.' She looked down at her hands for a moment, clearing her throat. 'What would you like me to bring? Drinks? Dessert?'

'Don't bring a thing.'

'But I have to.'

Her words were serious, absolute, and it took a moment for realisation to dawn on him. She needed to bring something, to feel as though she was contributing. Those were the rules of polite society and Stacey Wilton adhered to them. Pierce was probably more slap-dash, more than willing to take care of all the preparations and give Stacey the night off, as it were, but he could see that being told to do nothing was stressing her more than being asked to contribute. It reminded him of his mother—always busy, always willing to help, always putting others before herself—and for a moment a wave of nostalgia swept over him.

'In that case, how about dessert?'

She visibly relaxed, and Pierce was pleased to see the smile return to her face.

'Excellent. Dessert it is.'

'I'm looking forward to it.'

'You may regret saying that,' she said, chuckling and held up her hands. 'George likes making desserts, and his favourite colour is blue. Needless to say we've been having a lot of blue-coloured desserts of late, so don't say I didn't warn you.'

Pierce laughed at her words and nodded. He was about to reply when the bell which was over the front door to the clinic tinkled, alerting them to the fact that someone had just walked into the waiting room.

She checked her watch. 'A bit late.'

When Stacey started to rise from her chair he immediately held up a hand to stop her. 'Don't stress. I'll deal with it. You rest.'

As he headed off before she could protest Stacey watched his purposeful, long stride. So bold, as though he knew exactly where he was going in life and how he was going to get there. If that really was the case, she envied him.

Although as far as she was concerned she *did* know exactly where her life was headed—especially as Lydia was only seven years old. Stacey's life wasn't her own, and there was nothing she could do about it. Cora had her research into island diseases and her work in the Pacific island nation of Tarparnii to contend with, Molly was following her dream of becoming a general surgeon, and Stacey—dependable, sensible Stacey—was stuck at home raising her half-siblings.

She knew she shouldn't complain, and most days she was able to handle these negative emotions, but today, being asked out to dinner by a handsome man, and for one moment pretending that he was asking her and only her, had reminded her of what life had been like before her parents' death. That was the way things had been a few years ago when she'd met Robert, when he'd taken her to the most lavish restaurant in Perth, gone down on bended knee and proposed to her in front of an entire restaurant full of guests.

'I love you', he'd professed. 'Be my wife?'

Of course she'd said yes. She'd loved him. But the instant her father and stepmother had been so cruelly taken from them Stacey's life had all but disappeared, with everyone simply expecting her to take over. Unfortunately Robert hadn't anticipated Stacey and her sisters becoming the children's legal guardians. He hadn't been able to understand why the younger children hadn't gone to live with Cora or Molly, and when Stacey had informed him that they would all be staying together—that the younger children needed all of their older sisters, that they all wanted to grieve together—he'd been unable to comprehend it.

Robert had therefore made his own decision and decided to call off their wedding. Unfortunately, he'd forgotten to tell her he'd changed his mind until she'd turned up at the church, dressed in white, sad because her father wasn't there to give her away. The groomsman had briskly apologised to her and then handed her an envelope which Robert had given him only twenty minutes earlier. In the envelope had been a short and concise note in Robert's bold handwriting, informing her that he'd changed his mind. There had been no apology, no other explanation.

Stacey shook her head, clearing her thoughts and swallowing over the lump in her throat. She blinked back the few tears that were starting to sting her eyes and forced herself to take five soothing breaths. Of course, as she'd belatedly realised, there'd been far too many things wrong with their relationship—such as the way Robert had always made her second-guess herself, or made her feel guilty for ruining their scheduled dates because her clinic had run late.

During this last year and a half she'd scooped up what had been left of her dignity, finished off her contract with Perth General Hospital as an A & E consultant and decided that a more sedate pace of life was in order. Seeing her father's old Newcastle GP practice up for sale had been the godsend she'd been waiting for. It had been her dream job when she'd been an innocent fourteen-year-old, wanting to follow in her father's footsteps. With so many things going wrong she'd been determined to make *this* dream become a reality.

It was only because Cora and Molly had sup-

ported her, as they'd always done, that the dream
had even been realised. It hadn't been easy, uprooting the children and moving so late in the
year, but everyone had coped well except for Jasmine. She frowned as she imagined what Jasmine's retort might be when Stacey told them all
that they'd been invited over to Pierce's house
for dinner. But it was their first official invitation since moving here, and it would be good
for all of them.

Stacey had a hunch that Jasmine would be delighted to meet Nell—especially as the school
Jaz had attended in Perth supported integration
of children with disabilities. But when she finally arrived home that night, and sat down at
the dinner table to enjoy the delicious meal of
spaghetti bolognaise and salad which Molly had
prepared, Jasmine's reaction was exactly as pre-
dicted the instant Stacey told them all about the
invitation.

'I don't want to go!' Jasmine shouted.

'Well, *I* want to go,' Molly countered, giving
Stacey a wide, beaming smile and waggling her
eyebrows up and down as a means of indicating
that she thought Pierce was cute.

Stacey ignored her antics.

'How sweet of Pierce to invite us all. Sorry, Jaz.' Molly put her arm around her half-sister's shoulders and pressed a quick kiss to her cheek—a move Jaz wouldn't tolerate from Stacey. 'Looks as though you'll just have to stick it out and come too.'

'I'm old enough to stay home by myself,' she retorted hotly, slamming her knife and fork onto her plate. 'I'm not a baby any more.' As she said the words she glared at Lydia, who was innocently enjoying her dinner and not paying one bit of attention to her sister's tantrum.

'No one's saying you are,' Stacey returned, but no sooner were the words out of her mouth than Jasmine pushed her chair back from the table and ran off to her room. Stacey closed her eyes and sighed. 'If Jasmine really wants to be treated in a more adult fashion then she's going to have to accept the responsibilities of being a part of this family—and that means attending events and accepting dinner invitations rather than having tantrums.'

Molly nodded. 'I'll speak to her when I'm finished eating.'

'Thanks, Mol.'

They both knew Molly would get much further than Stacey. It was basic psychology. Jasmine needed someone to blame for all the pain she was feeling and Stacey had been chosen as the winner. Most of the time she was fine with that. She understood Jasmine far more than the young girl realised, and knew that time really would heal the wound of losing her parents. But sometimes being on the end of her sister's cutting words was difficult to cope with.

'So we're all going, then?' It was George who asked the question, looking expectantly at his big sister.

'We are, George,' she confirmed, and the little boy grinned. 'We also need to make a dessert, so would you be able to hel—?'

'I'll help. I'll help,' he volunteered quickly, and Stacey blew him a kiss of thanks.

'What about Flopsy and Andrew?' Lydia asked.

'Yes, the rabbits can come, too.' Both Lydia and George cheered at this news, the two of them having taken to their new pets with the utmost joy. 'And, speaking of which, don't forget to feed them before you head off to brush your teeth.'

'Yes Stacey,' George and Lydia said in unison.

'Will we meet his sister?' George continued.

'Pierce's sister? Yes. Her name is Nell.'

'Nell.' George tried the name out. 'I like meeting new people.'

'Me, too,' Lydia agreed, slurping spaghetti into her mouth.

'Me three,' said Molly, following suit and slurping her own spaghetti—but not before giving Stacey a little wink. It was code for *Everything will work out fine. Stop stressing, sis*.

Stacey relaxed a bit and was pleased when, the following day, she was able to formally accept Pierce's invitation.

'Excellent,' he said. 'Nell's super-excited. She wanted to know why you all weren't coming over tonight, as she doesn't want to wait until tomorrow.'

Stacey chuckled as she made them both a cup of coffee. 'She wants to see the rabbits, doesn't she?' she stated. 'Flopsy and Andrew will be coming, too, so please reassure Nell.'

'Andrew?' Pierce raised an eyebrow.

Stacey shrugged. 'Lydia named him. She said he looked like an Andrew.' She chuckled and finished stirring their coffees.

'Lydia sounds like quite a character.'

'Oh, she is. Determined to be an actress or an astronaut. At the moment she can't decide, but her determined spirit never wavers.'

Pierce laughed as he gratefully accepted the coffee. 'I can't wait to meet her and the rest of your posse.' It was true. He had a sense that meeting the rest of the people who mattered most to Stacey would help him piece together more of the puzzle surrounding her.

'Posse?' She joined in his laughter, amazed at how light and free she felt, even though they had another hectic clinic scheduled. To have these few moments with Pierce was like a recharge for her internal battery. 'I just hope the noise we naturally generate doesn't scare Nell.'

'Thank you for being concerned about my sister's wellbeing,' he remarked after taking a sip of his coffee. 'I do appreciate it.'

This thoughtfulness of hers was yet another facet of Stacey's personality, and one he'd been aware of from their first meeting. She gave and she gave and she kept on giving to others, and it made him wonder just who in her life gave back to her. No doubt she was close to her sisters, but it sounded as though Molly was now super-busy and Cora was still overseas, so who did Stacey rely on for support? His natural protective instincts were increasing where Stacey was concerned and he was finding it difficult to stop thinking up ways he could help her.

They both stood at the kitchen bench, sipping their coffees, the silence quite companionable, so when the bell over the front reception door tinkled Stacey jumped, startled out of her reverie.

'Let's get Friday underway,' she remarked, quickly drinking the rest of her coffee and trying not to burn her tongue in the process.

'I'm really excited about tomorrow night,' Pierce said as they headed towards their consulting rooms. 'In fact, why don't you come over around four o'clock and Nell can show the children her puzzles. She's become quite good at sharing.' He straightened his shoulders, brotherly pride evident in his stature.

'That's great. Has it been difficult to get her to the point where she is happy to share her things?'

He shrugged one shoulder. 'It's been more of an ongoing thing all her life. Our mother was determined that Nell's autism would never be used as an excuse for bad manners, so Nell was taught from a young age the importance of being polite—and that included sharing. Like anyone, she has good days and bad days. But for the most part she no longer has a tantrum if people put a puzzle piece back in the wrong spot.'

'What does she do now if they do?'

'She waits until the person has finished playing with the puzzle and then she fixes it up before packing it away.'

'Good strategy.'

'It works. So—four o'clock sound good?'

She nodded. 'That gives us plenty of time to get crazy Saturday morning done and dusted and to organise the rabbits.'

'Crazy Saturday morning?'

'George goes to soccer, Lydia has ballet at eight o'clock and then gymnastics at ten, and Jasmine has a guitar lesson.'

'Guitar?'

'Electric guitar.'

'Oh, that sounds…fun—and noisy.'

Stacey grinned. 'Actually, she's pretty good.'

'She can bring her guitar if she likes. Give us an after-dinner concert, perhaps?' At Stacey's grimace he chuckled. 'Or not.' He stopped outside his consulting room door and placed a hand on her shoulder. 'Listen, if I don't get a chance to speak to you for the rest of the day, given just how hectic our clinics are, I'll see you tomorrow at four.'

Stacey was having a difficult time focusing on his words as the simple touch of his hand on her shoulder was enough not only to cause a deep warmth to flood throughout her entire body but for her mind to comprehend little of what he was actually saying. It had been so long since a man had been nice and kind and supportive, and it was…exciting.

Usually she just battled on with her day, her week, her life, sorting things out to the best of her ability, trying to make everyone around her happy. But at the moment it felt good to actually have Pierce standing by her side, offering his support. She had the sense that he was someone she could talk to and confide in. He also had an understanding of what it was like to raise a sibling—in her case more than one. Pierce had had to raise Nell after their parents had passed away, which couldn't have been at all easy.

Long after Pierce had dropped his hand from her shoulder the memory of his warm touch and the way his blue eyes had twinkled with calm reassurance were enough to get her through the rest of the day. However, by four o'clock the following afternoon Stacey's nerves were taut with stress once more.

Thankfully Molly had driven the short distance from their house to Nell's house, with the two rabbits safe in the cage on the back seat of the mini-van, placed between George and Lydia. Jasmine sat in the far corner, listening to her music on headphones and generally sulking.

'Is this where you used to live when you were little girls?' George asked as they climbed from the car.

'Yes,' Molly answered, handing Stacey the car keys as Stacey waited politely for Jasmine to precede her. The surly girl was clearly resenting being forced to come.

'You never know what's going to happen, Jaz,' Stacey said softly as Molly and the two children made their way up the path towards the front door, carefully carrying the rabbit cage. 'You might actually enjoy yourself. They really are very nice people. Especially Nell.'

As she spoke the words she sincerely hoped that Jasmine wouldn't kick up a fuss, because despite Pierce's reassurances she didn't want to test Nell's ability to cope with chaos.

With sullen steps and her arms crossed over her chest, Jasmine walked ahead of Stacey towards the front door. Stacey only remembered to lock the car at the last minute. She was a little disconcerted about their descending *en masse*, about her family creating too much noise, about seeing Pierce in a more social capacity. *No.* She wouldn't dwell on the latter. They lived and worked in a fairly close-knit community, and as doctors at the family medical practice it was only right that they become friends.

Nell stood at the front door with Pierce, formally welcoming everyone, even though Stacey could see that she was more interested in the rabbits.

'Please, come in to my home,' Nell invited warmly.

'Wow!' George and Lydia remarked as they stared at the ornate ceiling before doing a slow perusal of the room.

When Lydia spied the puzzles she relinquished her hold on the rabbit cage and raced over to where Nell had set them up on the floor. 'I love puzzles,' she declared, before tipping one over and starting to figure out how all the little wooden pieces went back in.

George continued his visual observation while Stacey introduced Jasmine to Pierce and Nell. The teenager managed the smallest glimpse of a smile when she shook hands with Nell.

'Right on time,' Pierce stated, grinning widely at Stacey.

She smiled back, feeling highly self-conscious and trying desperately to ignore the butterflies that had just been let loose in her stomach simply because she was in close proximity to him.

'Are you going to marry Stacey?' George asked, breaking the silence.

'What?' Stacey and Pierce said in unison.

CHAPTER FOUR

'GEORGE!' STACEY WAS gobsmacked. She looked at Pierce in shock, then back to her brother. 'What on earth made you say that?'

George stared at her with his big eyes—eyes that were so like their father's. 'Well…the last time we went to have dinner at a man's house was when you told us you was going to marry him.'

George's tone was a little indignant, and the puzzled frown on his face indicated that he wasn't sure what he'd done wrong.

'But then,' Lydia chimed in from the lounge room, where she was busy finishing off the puzzle, 'he decided *not* to marry you and you had to tell everyone in the church that he wasn't coming.'

'He didn't *want* you,' Jasmine added, and her words were spoken in a tone which was designed to hurt.

'Jasmine! That's cruel.' Molly's chastisement of the girl was instant. 'Apologise to Stacey.'

'What?' Jasmine spread both her hands wide. 'Why do *I* have to apologise and Lydia and George don't?'

'Because you know better,' Molly interjected.

Stacey watched the conversation going on around her—her siblings arguing, the rabbits getting agitated in their cage, Pierce looking back and forth between them all as if he was at a tennis match—and all she could focus on was her increased heart-rate hammering wildly against her ribs. She saw Jasmine's mouth move, the framing of an apology on her lips, but the sound of the words didn't register, only the thrumming of the blood reverberating in her ears.

What must Pierce think of them all! No sooner had they stepped over the threshold than a family squabble had erupted. If this was Jasmine's way of making them all wish they'd left her behind at home, then it was starting to work. Emotional punishment, especially from her siblings, was the one thing Stacey wasn't good at dealing with.

'Stacey? Stace?'

She was vaguely aware of Molly calling her name, but mortification at the situation was getting the better of her and before she knew what was happening Stacey had whirled around on her heel and exited the house. She walked quickly down the street, moving as though on automatic. For a moment she thought no one was following her, and was extremely grateful, but a second or two later she heard a deep male voice calling her name.

Stacey didn't stop, didn't look back, and even when Pierce fell into step beside her she didn't speak a word. Thankfully he didn't try and stop her, didn't ask her to slow down, didn't offer placating words. Instead he seemed content just to walk beside her, matching her fast pace with ease. When she turned down a small lane which led to the park, he simply continued on alongside her.

She made a beeline for the swings—her favourite. The equipment at the park had been upgraded since she'd been here last, but apart from that everything was exactly the same. The familiar childhood setting calmed her somewhat,

and when she finally sat down on the swing, instantly pushing herself up, she started to feel the
consuming tension abate.

Pierce sat beside her on the other swing, and
after watching her for a moment he followed suit
and started swinging back and forth, not bother-
ing to speak or initiate conversation. After about
five minutes of swinging to and fro in silence
Stacey started to slow down, her breathing more
natural, her head cleared of its fog. Pierce slowed
down as well and soon both of them were just
sitting on the swings, rocking slowly back and
forth.

'Sorry,' she ventured.

'No apology necessary.'

'I hope Nell's all right and that our silly sibling
squabbling didn't upset her.'

Pierce nodded. 'Nell will be fine. She was ab-
sorbed with the rabbits, eager to get them out of
their cage.'

'Good.'

'Wait a second.' Pierce held up one finger. 'Did
you say *siblings*? Squabbling *siblings*? George
and Lydia and Jasmine are your *siblings*?'

'Yes.' She looked at him with slight confusion, then her eyes widened slightly. 'I thought you knew that.'

'Nope. I thought they were your children—or at least that some of them were.'

She shook her head. 'Nope. We were seventeen when Jasmine was born, so I *could* have been old enough to be her mother. But my father married our nanny, Letisha, when Cora, Molly and I were thirteen.' Stacey looked down at the ground. 'My mother walked out, abandoned us, when we were almost five.'

'How terrible for all of you.'

Stacey shrugged. 'Letisha's the only real mother we can remember. She looked after us for so long, and then when Dad was finally divorced he could admit he had feelings for Tish.' Stacey smiled sadly. 'They died together in a car crash. I don't think my father could have survived being left alone again.' She kicked the ground with her foot and dragged in a breath. 'Anyway, by the time the three of us had finished medical school we had three new siblings: Jasmine, George and Lydia.'

'And now, with your father and your stepmother gone, you're raising your siblings.'

'Yes. Although the three of us share legal guardianship of the younger three on paper, I seem to have become the designated parent in practice. Though in fairness Molly and Cora are very helpful.'

'But you're the disciplinarian?' He nodded, understanding what she was saying. 'It's not easy to discipline a sibling.'

'No. It's not.' She sighed and shook her head. 'I know psychologically that Jasmine is just going through a phase, that she needs to take her grief out on someone and that someone is me—especially as I've just uprooted her from her school friends and brought her to the other side of the country. I know how she feels because that's exactly what my father did to me when I was fourteen. He took us from Newcastle to Perth.'

'But coming back home was the right decision?'

'I know it is. And I know Jasmine will forgive me one day, just as I forgave my dad. But I wish—' She stopped and gritted her teeth, trying to control the tears she could feel pricking behind her eyes.

'You wish what?' His words were soft and encouraging.

'I wish she *liked* me.' She spoke softly. 'Just a little bit. Just every now and then.' Stacey sniffed, still working hard to gain some sort of control over her emotions. 'At least she gets along with Molly, and Cora is splendid with her.'

'Except Cora's not here and Molly's embarking on a new career path, leaving *you* to carry the burden of a grieving, angry young girl.' Pierce nodded, completely understanding the situation. 'It's not easy when you're thrust into the parental role when all you'd rather do is be their sibling, comfort them and cry with them and not be expected to have all the answers.'

'Exactly.' She dragged in another calming breath. 'I just hope Lydia and George don't develop over-active hormones when *they* enter their teenage years. It's not an easy time for Jasmine. I understand that.'

'But she has to realise that this isn't an easy time for you either. How long is it since your parents passed away?'

'Eighteen months.'

'Well, that's not going to be easy for any of

you—regardless of how old you are. Plus, it sounds as though you've had more going on than just the loss of your parents…at least from what George said.'

'Being jilted at the altar, you mean?' There was no point in beating about the bush, especially now, thanks to her siblings and the way they'd blurted out her past hurts.

He stared at her for a second. 'Oh, Stacey. What an idiot.'

'You weren't to know.'

Pierce reached over and took her hand in his. It seemed like the most natural thing in the world so she let him. Warmth spread up her arm and somehow filled her entire being, right down to the tips of her toes, and she just let it. Right at this moment she was tired of always being in control, of bottling up her own emotions and private thoughts.

'No, not me. *Him*. What an idiot he was to let you go.'

Stacey looked at her small hand sitting inside his big one. 'How could you possibly know that?' Her tone was soft, her words tinged with confusion. 'You barely know me.'

'I met you three weeks ago, Stacey, and although I don't profess to know *everything* about you the essentials of your personality are quite clear.'

'They are?'

He gave her a lopsided smile and she had to work hard to calm the butterflies in her stomach. It was bad enough that the touch of his skin against hers was causing her heart-rate to increase. Did she have no control over her senses where Pierce was concerned?

'Stacey, from the way you stood on the opposite side of the road, gazing with fond nostalgia at the house, I knew you were someone who had a big heart. The memories the place clearly holds for you are important, and you didn't shy away from that.'

She stared at him for a moment, then glanced down at their hands, at his thumb gently rubbing over the backs of her knuckles. She wished he'd stop, but at the same time she wished he'd never stop. Was he feeding her a line? Was he being nice to her because he wanted something from her? If so…what?

It had taken her quite a while to figure out that

Robert had had his own agenda when it came to their…union. He'd wanted a smart, pretty wife—someone who understood his work and who was dedicated to helping him climb the career ladder. What he *hadn't* wanted was an instant family.

'And if you want more examples of how I know your character,' Pierce continued, his tone as intent as his words, 'let's start with your concern for Edna and Mike, or of the way you talked about sitting in the bay window sharing your secrets with your sisters. But most importantly for me it was the way you interacted with Nell. As far as I'm concerned that's always the biggest indicator of a woman's true nature, because the instant a woman discovers I'm guardian to my little sister, and not only that but she has a learning difficulty, it's usually enough to make them head for the hills.'

'A *woman's* true nature?' she couldn't help quizzing.

It wasn't until Pierce looked into her blue eyes that he realised she was turning the tables, lightening the atmosphere, wanting to remove the spotlight from herself.

'There's a story there,' she said.

Pierce nodded and slowly let go of her petite hand. 'Of course there is, and it's one which has been repeated time and time again.'

'Which begs the question have *you* ever come close to matrimony?'

He nodded. 'I was engaged. Catherine was her name.'

'Was?'

'Still is, actually. She's alive and well, but—'

'But she couldn't take the responsibility of being guardian to Nell?'

Pierce shook his head. 'No. No, quite the opposite, actually.'

'Really?'

He exhaled slowly and looked down at the ground for a moment. 'Catherine was…*is*—' he glanced at her as he corrected himself '—the type of woman who loves to be of use. She loves helping others, being there for them. She's a brilliant doctor, ended up becoming an eye surgeon, but I guess the best way to describe her is that she needs to be needed.'

'So when she found out you had a sister with a disability she was happy about that?'

'Yes, and I thought, *Wow, here's a woman who likes me, who likes Nell, who loves being with both of us, who understands what we're about.*'

'What went wrong?'

Pierce paused. 'She accepted a job overseas, working with Pacific Medical Aid like your sister Cora.'

'Was this before or after your engagement?'

'It was two weeks before our wedding?'

'She just went overseas?'

'She said that we didn't need her as much as other people needed her. That being married would tie her down, would stop her from reaching her true potential which was to help as many people as she could.' Pierce met Stacey's gaze. 'Hard to argue with someone who only wants to do good in this world.'

'And is she doing good?'

'I believe she's presently in Iran, giving the gift of sight by performing cataract operations on those who otherwise could never afford it.'

'She sounds like quite a woman.'

He nodded. 'She sends me a Christmas card every year.'

'It's good that you keep in touch.'

'It is.' He nodded.

Stacey watched him for a moment, wondering if he still had feelings for Catherine. It was clear from the way he spoke of her that he admired her. Could she ask? They were being quite open with each other so why not?

'Do you…?' She hesitated for a moment, then took a breath and plunged right in. 'Do you still have feelings for Catherine?'

'Friendship feelings? Yes. Romantic feelings? No. But I wish her every success and happiness.'

'And yet you sound so forlorn.'

'I do?' He sat up straighter and chuckled. 'Sorry. I'm supposed to be the one cheering you up.'

'Then consider me cheered. You have performed your friendship duties well.'

'Friendship?' he queried.

'Isn't that why we're having dinner tonight? To build friendships not only for Nell but for each other?'

Pierce angled his head to the side. 'I guess I hadn't thought of it like that.'

'Perhaps because you're always so busy considering Nell's needs first and your own second.'

'I'm sure you know all about that, what with having so many siblings. But I think we could definitely be friends.' He spread his arms wide. 'We're off to a good start. We're swinging together.' He winked, implying a cheeky *double entendre*.

She laughed. 'Literally.'

'Yes. So, *friend*, tell me something about you that a lot of people—*sans* siblings—wouldn't know.'

Stacey sighed thoughtfully for a moment, then nodded. 'I love cheesy music videos.'

'Huh? That *is* surprising.'

'They're just so funny. The over-acting, the bad colour saturation, the strange vision of the film-maker. Sometimes the videos have absolutely nothing to do with the lyrics, and that just makes it even more ridiculous and funny. Some of the ones from the eighties are classics—especially with special effects which were considered so cutting edge at the time but nowadays are completely woeful.'

Pierce nodded, as though seriously considering her words. 'Cheesy music videos? I'm beginning to understand the appeal.'

'OK. Now it's your turn. Tell me something not many people know about *you.*'

Pierce opened his mouth, hesitated, then closed it again.

'Come on,' Stacey urged. 'Friends share.'

He nodded, but exhaled and closed his eyes before confessing, 'I like...to sew.'

'Sew?'

'If I hadn't had a passion for medicine and helping people I would have been a fashion designer.'

'Really?' Stacey couldn't help but chuckle at this news. 'Are you being serious or are you pulling my leg?'

He kept a straight face for a whole five seconds before grinning. 'Pulling your leg. I like to garden.'

'Well, that's hardly a secret. Your whole neighbourhood can tell you like to garden simply by the way you attend to those flowerbeds.' She swung back and forth a little. 'I liked the sewing story better, but if you ever feel like bringing your gardening skills over to my house then please feel free. I do not have a green thumb whatsoever.'

'Perhaps I can give you some pointers. We could do some potting and planting and then head inside and watch cheesy music videos.'

Stacey laughed, unable to believe just how light and happy she felt. How was it that Pierce had not only been able to shift her bad mood but make her feel optimistic?

'Gardening lessons?' She nodded. 'I might actually look forward to them.'

He stood from the swing and held out his hand to her. 'I hope you do.'

Stacey accepted his hand, but as she stood from the swing she over-balanced slightly and fell towards him. Pierce moved quickly and caught her, with one strong arm about her waist.

'Uh…sorry.' Stacey placed her other hand on his arm to steady herself, trying to ignore the instant warmth which flooded her body, her senses shifting into overdrive as she breathed in his spicy scent.

'You all right?'

His words were soft, his breath fanning her cheek, and when she lifted her head and looked at him she realised just how close her face was to his. Her gaze dipped to look at his mouth, lingering for a second before returning to meet his eyes.

'Uh...' She sent commands to her limbs, telling them to move, her legs to support her, but the sluggish signals took a few seconds to be received. 'Yeah. Yeah, I should be fine.'

As she shifted her weight, Pierce continued to hold her hand. 'Did you twist your ankle? Hurt yourself?'

'No. I just stepped wrong. The ground's a little uneven.'

He smiled at her. 'OK.'

They took a few steps away from the swings before he released her, shoving his hands into the pockets of his jeans as they headed back down the path. Stacey racked her mind for something to say, trying to get her brain back into gear rather than fixating on the way being so close to Pierce had made her feel.

They'd been doing so well, chatting and sharing as friends. She didn't want to be aware of him. She wanted their relationship to be one of easygoing colleagues and friends. She didn't want to dream of him, to wonder what it might be like to have his arms holding her securely, to have him gazing down into her eyes, to have his lips pressed against hers.

'Uh…' She stopped and quickly cleared her throat, astonished that her voice had broken with that one brief sound. 'Um…will Nell be all right with you leaving her like this? I mean, she doesn't know any of my family and—'

'Nell will be fine. Part of her preparation for living independently has involved developing a sort of *script*, I guess you'd call it, for when a visitor comes round. But with two rabbits there for her to play with I doubt she's given anyone else a second thought.'

'Well, that's good.'

'Plus, I'm sure your sister Molly will have everything under control.'

'Probably better than I ever could.' She sighed, thinking of the way Jasmine responded so positively to Molly.

'I doubt that's true. One day soon Jasmine will realise everything you've done for her, she'll see you in a different light, and she'll appreciate you much more.'

They were almost back at the house by now and Pierce started to slow his pace. He wasn't sure he was ready to go inside to the noise and bustle just yet. Chatting quietly, intimately with Stacey had been relaxing, and he couldn't remember the last time he'd allowed himself to relax.

'Oh, I hope so.'

Stacey, too, didn't seem in any great hurry to re-enter the house, and they stopped just outside Edna and Mike's place.

Stacey looked up at the fading light of the balmy September day. 'Hopefully Jasmine's been able to engage Nell in conversation.' Stacey looked across at the house. 'I hate to see her hurting.'

'Of course you do. She's your little sister and she's been through some fairly intense life changes.'

'But George and Lydia seemed to have coped.'

'Because they're younger. Child-like comprehension is sometimes a godsend, and at other times, it's an enviable reality.' He leaned up against the fence between the two properties.

Stacey watched him in the late-afternoon light. 'Did Nell understand about your parents' death?'

'It took her a while, and sometimes she was

quite confused when she couldn't find them, or when she'd find me quietly crying because I missed them so much.'

Stacey pulled her lightweight cardigan around her and crossed her arms in front in an effort to stop herself from touching him. She wanted nothing more than to reach out and place a re-assuring hand on his arm or, worse, to throw her arms around his waist and hug him close, desperate to let him know that she really did understand exactly where he was coming from and what he felt. Just because they were adults, it didn't stop them from wanting to see their parents again.

'It can get rather wretched sometimes,' she agreed, surprised to find her voice catching on the words. 'I often wonder where I'd be now if my parents hadn't died…if I didn't have the children to constantly consider. No doubt I'd be stuck in a loveless marriage with Robert who, as it turned out, only wanted to marry me because I fitted all his criteria. He might have professed undying love for me, but it was only another lie to secure what he wanted.'

Pierce looked at her for a moment, then shook

his head. 'Yep. He was an idiot. What I mean is—and if I may be so bold, given I don't know the circumstances—your ex-fiancé sounds quite thick.'

Stacey's smile was instant. 'Thank you.'

Pierce held out an open hand towards her. 'I mean you're intelligent, caring, thoughtful and incredibly beautiful. What sane man *wouldn't* want you?'

Stacey wasn't sure what to say. His warm, sweet words washed over her, making her feel cherished…and she couldn't remember the last time she'd felt cherished—if ever. They stood there, simply looking at each other, drinking their fill. Butterflies started to churn again in her stomach as the atmosphere between them began to intensify. The need to draw closer to him, to touch him, was starting to become over-whelming, and when she edged a little closer to where he stood she found that he was doing the same.

His gaze flicked down to encompass her mouth before returning to her eyes. He opened his mouth to speak, but before he could say another word Edna's front door opened and she came running out, all in a frantic tizzy.

'Edna?' Stacey called, and the other woman yelped with fright, clearly not expecting to find two people chatting near the bottom of her driveway. 'Is something wrong?'

'It's Mike. He's got pains. I was just coming to get Pierce and call the ambulance,' she said, indicating the cell phone in her hand.

'I've got my big emergency bag in my car,' Stacey remarked, fishing her car keys from her pocket.

'Thanks,' Pierce called over his shoulder as he headed inside with Edna.

By the time Stacey joined him he'd placed Mike in the recovery position. He accepted a stethoscope from Stacey and listened to Mike's heart.

'Ambulance is on it's way,' he informed her as she wound the blood pressure cuff from the portable sphygmomanometer around Mike's arm.

'BP is elevated,' she responded a moment later. 'How do his lungs sound? Asthma?'

'Not asthma. Probably an angina attack.'

Pierce met and held her gaze for a moment, his eyes clearly saying, *Let's hope that's all it is.*

'I'm not…an…idiot,' Mike puffed, his eyes shut. 'Silence…speaks…volumes.'

'Shush, Mike,' Edna said, bossing him around. 'Let the doctors do their work.'

'You've always been very astute, Mike.' Stacey gently rubbed his arm, wanting to reassure him in any way she could. 'Try and focus on your breathing for me. Slow, calm breaths. We're going to set up an IV, just to get some fluids into you, so that by the time the ambulance arrives you'll be in a better state to receive further treatment.'

'What's…wrong?' he panted, reaching out for his wife's hand. Edna dutifully held it, but when she looked up at Stacey, there was fear in her eyes.

'We're not sure at this stage, Mike,' Pierce added as he reached into Stacey's well-stocked emergency bag, which was more like a huge backpack, pulling out the equipment they'd need for inserting an in vitro line into Mike's left arm. 'But rest assured Stacey and I will do everything we can to help.'

'Where is it painful?' Stacey asked Mike, and he told her the pain was down his right arm and across his chest. 'You're doing a good job of controlling your breathing. Well done. Is the pain constricting when you breathe in or out or both?'

'Both.'

'Is the pain stabbing or constant?' Stacey opened the tubing packet while Pierce inserted a cannula into Mike's arm.

'Constant.' He paused. 'Sometimes stabbing.'

'Any other pain? Headache? Tingling in your legs?'

'No.'

'Good.'

By the time they'd finished inserting the drip, Edna still sitting by her husband's side, holding his hand as though she was never letting go ever again, they could hear ambulance sirens in the distance.

Pierce looked across at Stacey. 'Are you OK to hold the fort for a moment? I just want to check on Nell. No doubt the sirens are going to bring the others out to see what's going on.'

'Good point.' Stacey nodded, and wasn't surprised to find Molly walking into Edna and Mike's house less than three minutes later.

'Mike? Mike?' Molly knelt down by his side. 'Ah…look at this. Stacey's got you all ready for the ambulance. Isn't she great?'

'She really is,' Pierce remarked as he re-entered the house. 'Ambulance is just pulling into the driveway. Time to get you mobile.' Pierce ran through what would happen, so Mike and Edna were completely aware of the procedure.

'I can go with him, can't I?' Edna asked as Stacey performed Mike's observations once more, pleased to announce that his BP was starting to level out, thanks to the IV drip.

'That's good news,' Pierce told him as the paramedics came into the house.

Stacey spoke with Molly, making sure her sister was all right to stay with Nell and the children.

'They've spent a lot of time playing with the rabbits and they're just sitting down to do some puzzles. Jasmine's been really good with Nell.'

Stacey sighed with relief. 'I was hoping she would be.'

'George and Lydia are having a turn with the rabbits in the back yard,' Molly continued, talking as though she was giving a patient debrief. 'And I've checked the kitchen—Pierce has pre-cooked an amazing meal, so I'll save you both some and we'll just get on with our night of getting to know Nell.'

'Sounds like a good plan,' Pierce remarked. 'Once Mike's all settled we'll head back.'

'Agreed.' With a brisk, formal nod that would serve her well in the surgical world, Molly kissed both Edna and Mike on the cheek before heading next door.

After they'd assisted the paramedics in settling Mike in the ambulance, Edna rode along with him and Stacey and Pierce followed in Stacey's car. Stacey couldn't help but be impressed with Pierce's cool, calm and collected bedside manner. Mike hated fuss at the best of times, and to work alongside a doctor who could communicate with her via looks, nods or a brief well-chosen word was excellent.

It made her think about her long-term plans for Shortfield Family Medical Practice. At the moment there was enough work for one full-time doctor and one part-time doctor, but patients who had been fed up with seeing locums were now returning to the family-oriented practice, and that meant longer waiting lists. That wasn't what Stacey wanted. Even though Cora was due to return at the end of the year, chances were they would soon be requiring more than two doctors to work at the clinic—especially as she already had plans for Winifred, their nurse-receptionist, to start conducting immunisation clinics.

Pierce seemed the obvious choice to approach with regard to a partnership. He would be close to Nell and could keep an eye on her, he was amazing with the patients and he worked exceptionally well with her. Good doctors were hard to find, so she accepted the silent challenge to persuade Pierce to stay permanently at Shortfield Family Medical Practice.

Of course there was the added advantage that he was dreamy to look at, that he made her laugh and that he could ignite an instant fire deep within her. But that was completely beside the point…wasn't it?

CHAPTER FIVE

THANKFULLY, DUE TO their prompt action, Mike was only in hospital for six days, admitted for a mild myocardial infarction.

'You were lucky this time,' stated Brian, the cardiac specialist at Newcastle General. 'But it means big changes, Mike.'

Mike groaned. 'I don't have to eat those fat-free bran muffins Edna keeps wanting to force down my throat, do I?'

Stacey chuckled at her friend's resigned tone. Pierce joined in and she looked across at him. They'd both known Mike was going to be discharged that morning, so had come to listen to what the specialist had to say and also to offer moral support to both Edna and Mike. Going to hospital could be scary enough, but sometimes being discharged could be equally unsettling.

'See? Even Brian's telling you to listen to me and to stop sneaking foods which are bad for you,' Edna chastised, before staring at Mike. 'I love you, Mikey. I need you.' She took his hand in hers. 'And if eating fat-free bran whatever means that I get to be with you longer, then that's what we'll eat. *Both* of us.'

Mike raised his wife's hand to his lips and kissed it, glistening tears in his eyes. 'That's what we'll do, love,' he finished.

Stacey couldn't believe how blessed she was to be witnessing such an intimate connection between her two friends. After over forty years together they were still deeply in love, and she immediately missed her own parents. When she glanced across at Pierce, who was on the opposite side of Mike's bed, she could almost sense that he felt the same as her, except about his own parents.

'Good to hear,' Brian continued. 'Besides, the only reason you're going home now is because Pierce lives next door to you and Stacey's going to check on you every day.'

'What about district nurses?' Edna queried. The consultant stared at Edna, then shook his head.

'Mike? Listen to a district nurse? I'd feel sorry

for the nurse.' Brian chuckled. 'From all those years of playing hockey and football with Mike, I know, Edna, that it's best if someone he loves comes and bosses him around—especially with regard to anything medical.' Brian placed a hand on Mike's shoulder. 'You're a cantankerous old man now, Mike. We both are. And it's best we take steps to protect others from ourselves.'

Mike grinned at his old friend. 'Too true.'

Stacey laughed and walked across to Mike's bedside and kissed his cheek. 'I love you, Mike,' she said. Then she whispered in his ear, 'And you're the closest thing I have to a father. *Please* take care of yourself. I need you.'

When she straightened her eyes were glistening with tears. She'd only meant to encourage him, and yet here she was, standing before the head of cardiology, blubbering.

Mike looked at her firmly, then took her hand in his and gave it a squeeze. 'I'll not let you down, girl,' he promised, his voice choking with a mixture of determination, sincerity and love.

Edna hugged Stacey. 'It's perfect timing that you're back. We need you and you need us. It's right that you're back where you belong.'

And that was exactly how Stacey felt as she walked into her clinic on Friday morning, four weeks after taking it over. Coming home to Newcastle *had* been the right decision, although Jasmine would probably disagree.

As she walked through the clinic, switching on various machines to warm them up, Stacey was surprised to find Pierce in his consulting room, given it had only just gone seven o'clock. She stopped by his open door. 'Good morning. You look as though you've been here half the night.'

He looked up from his computer screen and smiled at her as she walked in, coming to stand near his desk. 'No. Just half an hour or so. I was just finishing up an article I promised I'd write for the team at Yale.'

'Yale? Yale as in the prestigious American university?'

'Yes. Presently the team there are leading the world when it comes to understanding autism and autism spectrum disorders, but there's still so much we don't know about adult autism.'

'Which is where you come in?'

'Sort of.'

'As I've mentioned, I've read your articles. They're good.'

'Thank you.' He used the computer mouse and clicked a few times before switching off his monitor. 'At any rate, the article is now done and on its way to Professor Smith for his approval.'

'I'm sure he'll do more than approve. Have you worked with the Yale team for long?'

Pierce nodded as he stood from his chair, linking his hands behind his back and pulling downwards. Stacey tried not to stare.

'For quite a while.'

'I'm surprised they haven't offered you a job.'

'Well…' He shrugged, then lifted his hands over his head.

Stacey had been about to ask him some more questions, but the words didn't make it as far as her lips as all she was conscious of was the way his trousers dipped and his white and blue striped shirt rose up. He hadn't bothered to tuck it in and she was treated to a glimpse of his firm, smooth abdominals. Good heavens! Did the man work out every day?

She curled her fingers into her palms in an attempt to stop her itching need to walk over to him and feel just how firm those abs really were. Stacey swallowed, her lips parting to allow the pent-up air to escape, only then realising that her heart-rate had increased, and her breathing was more shallow than normal.

It wasn't until he lowered his hands, the shirt sliding back into place, that she realised she hadn't heard a word he'd said—if he'd said anything at all. Quickly she raised her gaze to meet his, hoping he hadn't noticed she'd been openly ogling him. He raised an eyebrow and she noticed a soft, slow smile tugging at the corners of his mouth. It wasn't a teasing smile but one of interest.

Interest? He was *interested* that she'd been ogling him? Mortification ripped through her and she quickly looked away.

'Stacey?'

She headed towards the door, unable to look at him. 'Yeah?'

'Stacey...'

His tone was a little more urgent and she

stopped in her tracks before glancing at him over her shoulder. She swallowed.

'Er...' She cleared her throat, unable to control her rapid breathing.

He walked over to her and stood quite near. She wished he hadn't, because as soon as she breathed in, hoping to gain some sort of control over her wayward senses, all she was aware of was the fresh spicy scent which surrounded him. That and the warmth emanating from him made for a heady combination. The breath she exhaled was jittery and, knowing it probably gave him every indication that she was highly aware of him, Stacey sighed with veiled embarrassment and closed her eyes.

What must he think of her? First she'd ogled him and now she was behaving like a complete ninny, all flustered by his nearness. Her mind had gone completely blank—except for the image of him standing there, stretching his arms above his head.

'Stacey?'

'Hmm?' Her eyes snapped open and she realised with a start that he'd actually moved closer than before. When he reached out a hand and tucked a lock of hair behind her ear she gasped, her body starting to tremble not only at his nearness but at the way he'd touched her with such tenderness.

His fingers trailed slowly down her cheek. His gaze firmly locked with hers. It was as though they were in their own private world, just the two of them, time standing still. With her heartbeat thrumming wildly within her ears, she idly wondered if he could hear it.

'Your hair is so soft.'

His words were barely a whisper, but they made her tremble with the realisation that perhaps she wasn't the only one experiencing emotions of awareness. Then again, maybe Pierce gave out random compliments to women as part and parcel of his personality.

'Erm…thank you.' Her words were a little stilted, due to the lack of oxygen reaching her brain simply because of his touch. She needed to move, needed to put some distance between them, and when Pierce dropped his hand back to his side, still staring at her as though he wanted nothing more than to stand there and look into her blue eyes for the rest of the day, she forced herself to edge back.

Unfortunately she hadn't realised how close she was to the door frame and bumped into it.

'Oops.'

'Are you OK?' He put out a hand to steady her.

Stacey cleared her throat and nodded, not trusting her voice not to betray the way he made her feel. She jerked her thumb over her shoulder, indicating the hallway leading to the kitchen. Pierce smiled, as though he knew exactly what was going on, as though he understood exactly why she was unable to speak, and by the delight which was still in his eyes it appeared he really didn't mind at all.

Stacey turned, sighing harshly—more at her own foolishness than anything else—and made her way to the kitchen. Coffee. If she had a coffee perhaps she'd be able to think more clearly.

She sensed rather than felt him following her, so abruptly changed her mind and took a detour into her consulting room. Now that she didn't have his hypnotic scent winding its way around her, or the warmth of his body so near to her own, or the touch of his fingers sliding through her shoulder-length brown hair, Stacey rebooted her brain and forced herself to speak as though nothing out of the ordinary had just happened.

'I'll just put my bag down,' she called.

'Right. I'll switch the coffeemaker on so it can warm up,' he returned.

She almost laughed at the absurdity of their conversation. Polite, professional, impersonal. They were colleagues and new friends, and none of that meant they should be staring deeply into each other's eyes like lovestruck teenagers!

After taking a few calming breaths, Stacey squared her shoulders and walked into the kitchen, determined to focus on one thing—coffee.

'Is the machine ready yet?' She barely spared him a passing glance as she went to the fridge for the milk, noticing he'd already placed two cups on the bench.

'Stacey—what just happened?'

She turned and glared at him, almost dropping the milk. 'What do you mean?'

Pierce waved one hand in the air. 'You ogled

me. I caressed your hair. Surely you haven't forgotten already?'

She closed her eyes for one long moment, trying to suppress the tingles and nerves and flutterings of desire she could feel returning. The coffee machine dinged, signifying that it was ready to use. Glad of something to do, Stacey worked on automatic pilot to produce two coffees, adding milk to her own and letting him sugar his coffee himself.

'Like any normal person, when they experience a situation which makes them feel mildly uncomfortable and self-conscious, I *had* planned to forget it, actually.' She forced herself to meet his gaze, even though it was incredibly difficult, and was proud of herself for accomplishing the task. 'Clearly you feel otherwise. So—all right—let's discuss it.'

'Are you always so amenable to doing what everyone else wants?' Pierce stirred sugar into his drink, watching her closely.

'What do you mean?'

'Well, you don't want to talk about those amazing few moments when I invaded your personal space and lost all self-control by touching your hair, and I do.'

As he spoke Stacey felt the fire she'd only just managed to get under control ignite again. They'd known each other for almost a month now, had been working side by side. They'd cared for their patients, met each other's families, shared meals together and she'd learned a lot about him in such a short space of time—especially about the way he treated others. She had to admit that Pierce was quite a man when it came to conversing easily...just as he was doing with her now. The way he could so openly admit that he wanted to touch her hair, be so self-assured, was an admirable quality.

'What I want,' Stacey finally replied as she picked up her coffee cup and held it in front of her, as though she could hide behind it, 'is to take the shortest possible route back to rational thought, which will undoubtedly promote a comfortable working atmosphere. Hence why I was going to push the...you...invading...personal space thing...to the back of my mind and pretend it never happened.'

Pierce leaned a little closer, invading that barrier again. 'But it did.'

His rich, deep baritone caused vibrating tingles to flood through her.

'What if I want to touch your hair again? What if I want to caress your beautiful smooth skin?'

He breathed out slowly, his words unhurried, and she found it difficult to look away from his hypnotic gaze. Was that what he wanted to do? Really?

'What if I want to run my thumb over your lips...?' He stared at her mouth for a good few intoxicating seconds as he continued to speak. 'What if I want to watch them part with the anticipation of feeling my lips pressed against them?'

Her eyes widened at his words and she couldn't help flicking her gaze between his mouth and his eyes, wondering if he was being serious, wondering if he was just teasing, wondering if he actually meant every word he was saying and was about to follow through with a demonstration. The nervous knots caused by his close proximity and her secret need to have him do exactly as he said tightened in her belly.

It *was* there. The attraction she'd been trying to fight could no longer be denied—not now that he'd spoken so openly about it.

Her tongue slipped out to wet her pink lips and she watched as Pierce's gaze took in the process. A slow, deep sigh was drawn from him. He stood there for another half a minute, his jaw clenching a few times, as though he was trying desperately to control some inner urge—even though he was still invading her personal space, still holding his coffee cup in front of him as though in need of protection from his own emotions, just as she was.

'But you're probably right,' he remarked in his normal tone, before swallowing a few times, his Adam's apple working its way up and down his throat above his open-necked shirt. He took two steps back, determined and surefooted. 'Perhaps it *is* best if we ignore this attraction…'

He gave her a lopsided grin which did absolutely nothing to settle her nerves.

'At least for now. Winifred will be in soon, as will our plethora of patients, and we both have work to accomplish before that happens.'

Then, with a nod, he turned and walked from the kitchen, whistling as though nothing untoward or life-changing had just happened. Stacey watched him go with a mixture of confusion, uncertainty and heightened sensuality.

She shook her head. 'What on earth just happened?'

As though by some unspoken mutual agreement, Stacey and Pierce kept their distance from each other for the rest of the day. Friday clinic sessions were usually hectic, and that evening when she finally arrived home after finishing off the paperwork, long after everyone else had left, Stacey collapsed onto the sofa.

'Whatcha doin', Stace?' Lydia asked as she came over and sat on her sister.

'*Ugh*. What have you been eating?' Stacey asked as she pulled the girl into her arms. 'You're so heavy.'

'Jaz bought us chicken schn—'

'Schnitzel,' Stacey supplied.

'With vegetables from the chicken shop. It was super-yum. There's a plate of food for you and

Molly. George and I put it together and put some plastic wrap on it.'

'Thank you, Lyds.' Stacey hugged her sister. 'How grown-up of you.'

'George and I ate at the table, but Jaz got angry at *nothing* and took her dinner to her room.'

Stacey frowned at this news, making a mental note to check Jasmine's room later on, hoping to find an empty plate. This wasn't the first time Jasmine had taken her food to her room to eat. It had started a month or two after their parents' death. Molly had wondered whether their sister was in danger of anorexia or bulimia, but Cora had assured them both that Jasmine was eating. However, since Cora had left for Tarparnii Jasmine had become even more withdrawn. Stacey guessed that *any* change—and Jasmine had certainly had a few—was difficult for her to cope with.

'Why is she like that? Angry at nothing?' Lydia asked, her words filled with innocent confusion. 'Am I gonna be like that when I become a teenager?'

Stacey smiled and kissed Lydia's cheek. 'No. You might get a little moody every now and then, but Jaz is…confused. She can't understand why Mum and Dad died.'

'I can. It's because the angels needed help in heaven and they chose the two best people for the job.'

Stacey's eyes filled with tears at Lydia's words. She hugged her sister close again, wanting to absorb that innocence and hold onto it for as long as possible.

'That's beautiful, Lyddie,' Molly said from the doorway, instantly coming over to kneel on the floor beside the sofa.

'It is,' Stacey replied.

Lydia scrambled out of Stacey's arms and flung herself at Molly. 'There's chicken schnotzel in the kitchen. George and I made a plate of food for you and Stacey.'

Molly hooted with laughter and stood, whizzing Lydia around in her arms. 'Schnotzel, eh? Thank goodness you kept it safe. Come on, Stace. We'd best go eat our schnotzel.'

Stacey giggled as she hefted herself from the sofa, feeling less exhausted than when she'd walked through the door. Glad it was Friday night and she could stay up a bit later, Lydia went off to play with George while the two women sat eating in peace.

Molly looked closely at her sister. 'So… Interesting day?'

'Full day. Lots of patients. Lots of hay fever and sinus problems. Plus there seems to be a gastro bug making the rounds.'

'Yeah. A few bad cases came in to the hospital when I was in the emergency department just before I left—although it could have been food poisoning. I'll check later on, when I head back.'

'You're on call tonight?'

Molly shook her head. 'Just early tomorrow morning. Split shift. The work of a surgical registrar is never done—which is why, when we get the time, we high-tail it back home to enjoy some chicken schnotzel for dinner and to catch up on sleep. And we don't feel at all sorry for the poor doctors we leave behind to cope—like Pierce.'

'Pierce?' Stacey sat up a little straighter in her chair. 'He's doing a shift in the ED tonight?'

'Yeah. He said someone wanted to switch with him and he was fine with that.'

'He's doing a night shift?'

'Yes. What's the problem with that?'

'Oh. Nothing. He was just in very early this morning at the clinic.'

Molly raised an inquisitive eyebrow. 'Worried about the man's sleeping habits?'

Stacey looked down at her meal, knowing if she kept looking at Molly she'd soon be spilling the beans about what had occurred between them that morning. 'He's an employee…sort of. So of course I'd be concerned about his lack of sleep. I mean, I wouldn't want him doing house calls or treating patients when he's half asleep, now, would I?'

'No. No. Of course not.'

Molly stared at her sister and Stacey looked back across at her.

'What?'

'Is that the *only* reason why you're so concerned about him?'

'Yes.' The word was high-pitched, and sounded false even to her own ears.

'Or is it because the two of you…shared a moment?'

Stacey's eyes widened. 'How could you *possibly* know that?' she squeaked, her knife and fork clattering to her plate. She leaned forward and said in a softer tone, 'What did he tell you? What did he say?'

Molly grinned wildly at her sister and slowly forked another mouthful of chicken into her mouth. She chewed with equal slowness and swallowed before shaking her head from side to side. 'Pierce didn't say anything. You just confirmed a hunch I had—especially after watching the two of you together last weekend at dinner. You were both so cute, so friendly, but with… something more buzzing between you which neither of you wanted to acknowledge.'

'Molly!'

'And then tonight,' Molly continued, as though Stacey hadn't protested, 'he told me three times what a great doctor he thinks you are. He's too much of a gentleman to kiss and tell.'

'There was *no* kissing,' Stacey pointed out.

'But you wanted there to be, didn't you?'

It wasn't a question, it was a statement, and Stacey realised there was no way in the world she could pull the wool over her sister's eyes. Molly knew her as well as she knew herself.

She felt all the fight seep out of her. There

seemed no point in denying there was an attraction existing between Pierce and herself. She sat back in her chair and momentarily covered her face with her hands, nodding in affirmation. 'I *did* want him to kiss me. Oh, Molly.' She stared at her sister. 'What am I going to do?'

CHAPTER SIX

AS PIERCE SAT at the nurses' station in the Emergency Department, glad of a quiet night so far, he couldn't help but think of the way he'd actually touched Stacey's hair that morning. What he'd told her had been the truth—he'd thought about touching her hair from the first time he'd seen her. It had looked so soft and glossy in the sunshine that day, as it had bounced around her shoulders, her fringe framing her face perfectly.

He'd been determined to keep his distance, to ensure that his relationship with Stacey remained one of a working friendship. But the night her family had come for dinner, the way he'd felt the need to follow her to the park to ensure she was safe, then having her open up to him about her life, had only intrigued him even more.

Who *was* Stacey Wilton? The *real* Stacey Wilton? What were her dreams and hopes for *her* future? He, of all people, knew what it was like to live for others, always putting your own life on hold for everyone else—and he only had one sibling to consider. Stacey had five.

After Mike's admission to hospital last week he and Stacey had returned to his house, where Molly had been in full organisational mode. It hadn't felt awkward, walking into Nell's house and seeing it full of other people. It had felt right, somehow. It hadn't felt awkward eating the dinner he'd prepared and which Molly had reheated, sitting alongside the sisters, all of them chatting quietly but happily. It hadn't felt awkward when he and Stacey had rinsed the plates and stacked the dishwasher, tidying the kitchen together. Everything had felt...*right*.

Along with that, Nell had loved spending time with the rabbits, and she had definitely formed a bond with George, Lydia and especially Jasmine. Pierce had discovered that out of the Wilton triplets Stacey was indeed the oldest—'By five minutes,' Molly had told him. 'And she never lets us forget it.'

He'd liked watching the easy interaction between the sisters. The tight bond they shared was quite evident. Still, all he could see was Stacey, giving her time to everyone else. Accommodating Cora's desire to head off to work as a doctor in Tarparnii. Encouraging Molly's desire to study surgery. Assisting George and Lydia as they entered the world of raising a championship rabbit jumper.

'She's quite a woman, our Stace,' Mike had said one evening, when Pierce had dropped by to check on him, and had been pleased with the other man's progress. 'She's always putting others ahead of herself. For as long as I can remember—even when she was little.' Mike had thrown some poker chips onto the table. 'I call.'

'We often worry—especially after what that terrible Robert did to her.' Edna's indignation was fierce. 'She stood at the front of that church, wearing her wedding dress, calmly told everyone there wouldn't be a wedding and apologised for any inconvenience. Molly or Cora would've been happy to make the announcement, but Stacey insisted on doing it, on making sure they didn't have to bear her burden.' Edna shook her head. 'Goodness knows whether she'll ever get married now.' She looked at her cards. 'I fold.'

'It'll be tough for her,' Mike added. 'Those kids need a stable environment, and she's doing her best to provide it for them.' Then he pointed to Pierce's cards. 'You gonna call or fold, boy?'

Pierce looked absent-mindedly at his cards, more focused on the way Stacey was constantly infiltrating his thoughts rather than on playing the game. He'd already realised she was the type of woman to put others before herself, and it made him want to do something nice for her— something unexpected, something *just for her.* But what? 'Uh…fold.'

Mike shook his head. 'Easy victory. Your mind's not on the game tonight, boy.'

'I'll go put the kettle on,' Edna said as she stood from the table and headed into the kitchen. 'You go sit in your comfy chair, Mike. Time to put your feet up!' she called.

'Yes, dear,' Mike replied, and rolled his eyes. 'Help an old man up, Pierce.'

'You're not that old,' Pierce protested, but still did as he was bid.

'She's tying you in knots, isn't she?'

The question was rhetorical and Pierce looked at Mike with a frown.

'Oh, don't give me that. I've seen the two of you in the same room together—those sneaky little looks you both have. You like her. She likes you. I get it. I've been there, too, you know. Might have been a long time ago, but my Edna had me in a right tailspin and I had no idea how to pull out of it.'

'How *do* you pull out of it?' Pierce asked as he tucked a blanket around Mike's legs and made sure the television remote controls were within easy reaching distance.

Mike laughed, then coughed. 'Sometimes, boy, you've gotta fly right through it. No pulling up, no manoeuvring around it. Gotta go through it.'

Pierce shook his head. 'I've been down that road, though. It didn't end well.'

'Your fiancée left you and broke your heart—but that was a while ago and you're over it now. Edna told me.'

'Edna has a way of getting information out of people.'

Mike grinned. 'That's my girl.' He rested his head back and closed his eyes. 'So you're not gonna do anything about the way Stacey makes you feel?'

'I don't know.' Pierce paused, then looked at his friend. 'I've been head-hunted by a hospital in America.'

Mike opened his eyes. 'Really?'

Pierce smiled. 'Edna didn't manage to wheedle *that* titbit out of me.'

'What about Nell?'

'That's why I've spent so long setting up her independent living situation. Her new housemates will move in soon, and Nell's ready for that. She wants to do it. She knows I'll be overseas. We'll talk over the internet, and she'll have a network of people around her who are available whenever she needs them.'

Mike thought this over. 'How long are you going for?'

Pierce shrugged. 'At least six months—*if* I take the position.'

'When did they offer it to you?'

'Four years ago.'

'What?'

'I keep turning them down. They keep offering.'

'They must want you to work with them badly?'

Pierce nodded. 'They do.'

'Do you want to go?'

'Yeah, but—' He spread his arms wide. 'And that's always been the problem. There's always been a "but".'

'So for years you've not been able to go because of Nell?'

'Correct.'

'And now that Nell is finally settled and all ready for you to leave you're not sure because…?'

'Because what if this attraction between Stacey and myself is more than just an attraction? What if this is it? The one! What if she's the woman I'm meant to spend the rest of my life with?' Pierce began pacing up and down in front of Mike, then stopped and spread his arms wide again. 'Do you see my dilemma?'

Mike shrugged. 'You've put those Americans off for four years, laddie. What's a few more months? You've promised Stacey you'll stay until Cora gets back and you're not going to leave her in the lurch. It's not your way. So why don't you see whether this thing between you and Stacey *is* real? Give it a chance.'

'And what if it is? Does that mean I *never* get to go to the States?' Pierce raked both hands through his hair. 'Everything was going along just fine. I should have known that that would be when I finally met the woman of my dreams.'

'Your dreams, eh?' Mike chuckled. 'Then you've got nothing to worry about.' His grin widened as Edna came back into the room, carrying a tea tray. 'Dreams always come true.'

'Pierce…? Hello…?'

Sister was snapping her fingers near his face and Pierce instantly looked at her. 'Sorry. I was miles away.'

'Daydreamer!' She chuckled. 'Can you review these notes, please? Plus we've just had another drunk brought in by the police. Non-abusive, passed out in the middle of the road. I've put him in Cubicle Twelve.'

'Thanks.'

Pierce took the first set of case notes from the pile Sister had handed him and tried desperately not to think about the way he'd felt when he'd caught Stacey ogling him. Her visual caress, the way she'd responded when he'd touched her hair, when he'd later leaned towards her, looking deep into her eyes and realising he'd never felt that alive for years… Just that one moment…it had been intoxicating. It was also why he'd forced himself to walk away. Too much of a good thing could cause an addiction. But perhaps Mike was right. Perhaps he *should* give this attraction with Stacey a chance, see exactly it might lead.

The thought excited him and he smiled, thinking of what he might say to her the next time they met. If they had another tension-filled moment like the one they'd shared that morning he was determined that he wouldn't be the one to walk away. He wanted to know what it was like to kiss Stacey—well, perhaps it was about time he found out.

The insistent ringing of Stacey's cell phone woke her with a start. She sat bolt upright in bed and, having had years of practice at being instantly awake, quickly connected the call, her voice sure and firm—as though it *wasn't* half past two in the morning and she *hadn't* been sound asleep.

'Dr Wilton.'

'Stacey? It's my Gary. There's something wrong. I think he's eaten something, but he has a temperature and he's vomited, and I wasn't sure whether I should ring the ambulance because he's refusing to see a doctor, saying it's just food poisoning, but this is really bad and I didn't know what to do, and—'

'It's fine. Give me your address. I'll come over now and assess him,' Stacey interrupted, and quickly wrote down the details with the pen and paper she always kept on the bedside table. Initially she'd had no idea who Gary was, because her mind had still been coming out of the fog from her dream…a dream in which a tall, dark and handsome Pierce had brushed her hair from her face, leaned forward, pressed his lips to hers, kissing her with such tender passion…

Even now, as she did her best to reassure Gary's wife Nanette—who, it turned out, had been at school with her—Stacey could feel her cheeks still flushed with heat from the memories floating around in the back of her mind. As she ended the call and dressed she tried desperately to focus her thoughts on Gary's symptoms, planning several strategies in order to cope with a variety of possible scenarios. If Gary hadn't been able to keep any fluids down then his electrolyte levels might be low and he might require hospitalisation.

Out in the family room, Stacey collected her fully stocked emergency medical backpack from the locked cupboard and left a message for Molly on the whiteboard to let her sister know she'd been called out. Then she collected her handbag and car keys before heading out, thankful that Nanette and Gary didn't live too far away.

'Sorry for calling in the middle of the night.'

Nanette rushed out to meet Stacey, her words tumbling from her mouth as Stacey collected her backpack from the car and both women headed inside the house, which was lit up like a Christmas tree. Nanette had her two-year-old daughter in her arms, the child clearly having been woken from her sleep with all the ruckus and was not happy about it.

'That's what family practices are for, Nanette. To form bonds with the community. Which way?' Stacey's tone was firm and direct, yet she was also trying to reassure Nanette. She needed her to be calm, but given what she could remember of her old school friend that might be impossible.

'I didn't know what to do,' Nanette dithered. 'And I couldn't remember the name of your partner at the GP practice, who I saw the other day when one of my kids was sick, so I called your practice number and the answering machine gave me a cell phone number, and it turned out to be yours, but then I wasn't sure whether to call the ambulance or just take Gary to hospital myself, but when I tried to move him, to get him closer to the front door, he groaned so badly that I started trembling, and—oh, Stacey, I'm so glad you're back in Newcastle. Help my Gary. *Please?*'

Stacey continued to follow Nanette through the house, heading to the bedroom at the back where she could hear Gary groaning.

'What's *wrong* with him?' Nanette kept asking, and Stacey had to use all her mental control to block the other woman out and remain calm as she introduced herself to Gary.

The man was lying quite still, sweating and clammy to the touch. Stacey pulled out her stethoscope and lifted Gary's shirt, talking him through what she was doing. She listened to the sounds of his stomach, not wanting to palpate the abdomen, given he was already in so much pain.

She asked him about the times he'd been ill, about the type of pain he was experiencing, and after she'd taken his blood pressure and temperature she pulled her cell phone from her pocket and called for an ambulance, letting them know her suspected diagnosis.

'Appendicitis!' Nanette's high-pitched shriek made their daughter start to cry and Nanette quickly jiggled the toddler up and down, whispering soothing words.

'Is there someone who can look after your children for you, Nanette?'

'Oh. Oh. Uh… Yes. OK. This *is* happening?'

'Yes, it is.' Stacey took Gary's temperature again. 'We'll have you sorted out in next to no time,' she told him, giving him something to help with the pain.

Within another twenty minutes Gary was being wheeled on an ambulance gurney towards Trauma Room One.

'What have we got?' a deep male voice asked as Stacey quickly washed her hands before pulling on a disposable gown and a pair of gloves.

She let the paramedics give the debrief as she tried desperately to ignore the way her entire body seem to fill with trembles at the sound of Pierce's tone, but it was impossible. She was so incredibly aware of him, of memories of the way he'd tenderly touched her hair, of the way he'd stared into her eyes, of the dreams she'd had of the two of them together, and as she turned to look at him a fresh round of excitement burst forth when he smiled brightly.

'Hello, Stace.' He seemed a little surprised to see her but his smile was wide and genuine. 'No sleep for you tonight, eh?' he said as he walked over to where Gary was being transferred from the paramedic's gurney to the hospital barouche.

'No. I'm Gary's GP, and his wife called me because she was concerned. I'll just see him through to diagnosis. It'll help his wife to feel more relaxed if she knows I'm helping to look after her husband.'

He nodded. 'Fine by me if it's fine by the hospital,' he stated.

'I'm registered here.'

'Excellent.' Pierce hooked his stethoscope into

his ears, ready to listen to the sounds of Gary's abdomen.

Stacey looked at her patient, pleased she'd been able to convince Nanette to go and wait in the patients' lounge as Gary had turned exceedingly pale.

'I think he's going to be sick again,' Stacey warned, and the nurses were on the ball with their assistance, attending to Gary as Pierce finished his consult.

'Right. Let's get some fluids into him, boost electrolytes, and an injection of Maxalon to help stop the vomiting. Cross, type and match. We also need to lower that temperature. Get the on-call surgical registrar down here.'

Stacey and the rest of the Emergency Department staff started carrying out Pierce's orders.

'Molly said there have been quite a few cases of food poisoning presenting at the Emergency Department?'

'That's correct. But in Gary's case I think it's something a little more sinister.' Pierce had come around the barouche and was once more listening to the sounds of Gary's abdomen.

'Definitely appendix?'

'Definitely,' he confirmed as the surgical on-call registrar walked into the room.

'What do we have?' he asked.

'Forty-five-year-old male,' Pierce began, giving the registrar a breakdown of Gary's vitals. 'Initial suspected food poisoning, but all symptoms indicative of appendicitis with possible signs of peritonitis. Bloods have been ordered, but I don't think we can wait too much longer for the results.'

'Right.' The registrar performed his own set of examinations, listening to the sounds of Gary's abdomen before nodding and hooking his stethoscope about his shoulders. 'OK, Gary. We're going to get you to Theatre as soon as possible.' He turned to Pierce and Stacey. 'I'll go see if I can find a theatre that's free and get the paperwork started. Next of kin?'

'Gary's wife is in the patients' waiting room. She's quite distraught,' Stacey supplied.

'And who are you?'

'I'm their GP.'

'Excellent. Fetch the wife from the waiting room so I can explain the operation to her and her husband and get the consent forms signed.'

Stacey nodded as the registrar left the room.

'Brisk and to the point,' Pierce murmured. 'Your sister has a much better bedside manner.'

'I'm sure he's a good registrar,' she offered as they watched the nurses perform Gary's observations once more.

'Oh, he is. There's no doubting that.' Pierce stood beside her, speaking softly so only she could hear. 'I'm just saying that you Wilton women have a certain way about you that makes everyone feel more…calm, more relaxed. It's nice.'

He smiled at her—that cute, sexy little smile that she was coming to adore. Then he winked.

The intimate action, as though linking them in their own private bubble, caused Stacey's heart-rate to instantly increase. How was it possible that with such a small gesture he was able to tie her insides into knots and make her tremble all over?

Stacey licked her lips and gave him a little smile in return, before lifting the curtain which afforded Gary and the team the privacy they needed and slipping through before Pierce

turned the rest of her body to jelly with another
of his full-watt smiles.

When she'd licked her lips his gaze had
dropped, taking in the action, before he'd looked
into her eyes for a brief second longer. It was
why she'd forced herself to move, to step away
from his presence—because that one look had
said so much. It had said that he wanted to hold
her close, that he wanted to feel her touch, that
he wanted to press his mouth to hers and take
them both on a ride that would send them soar-
ing to the stars.

Stacey took some deep breaths and gave her
hands a little shake as she headed to the patients'
waiting room. She needed to get her mind off
the way Pierce made her feel and on to the job
she needed to do—which was to care for her
patients. Ever since yesterday morning…when
he'd caressed her hair, when he'd gazed into her
eyes, when he'd stared longingly at her lips…
Stacey had been hard-pressed to think of anything but that.

Before entering the waiting room she mentally
picked up her thoughts of Pierce and shoved them
into a box, promising herself she'd take them out

later and pore over every nuance and action. For now, though, Nanette and Gary needed her at her best, supporting them and helping them. She entered the waiting room and was surprised when Nanette grabbed her and hugged her close. Stacey gave her old school friend a brief rundown on what was happening to Gary and told her that he'd need surgery.

'So I was right to call you?' Nanette blubbered as Stacey offered her yet another tissue.

'You were absolutely right. Now Gary can get the treatment he needs.'

'Can I see him?' Nanette asked.

'Of course. The surgical registrar needs to talk to both of you and Gary needs to sign the consent forms.'

Nanette grasped Stacey's hands firmly in her own. 'You'll stay with me, won't you?'

'Of course.'

At this news Nanette nodded and reached for another tissue, wiping her eyes and blowing her nose. She pasted on a bright smile. 'How do I look?'

'Like a woman who loves her husband,' Stacey returned, momentarily envious of the connection Nanette and her husband had.

Why hadn't she realised sooner that Robert's words, his professions of love and his actions, hadn't exactly matched up? Perhaps it had been because she'd been desperate to make a connection, to try and find the sort of love that her father had found with Letisha. She'd believed in things that hadn't been there, she'd made excuses for Robert's behaviour, telling herself that he was stressed from working so hard in his pursuit of becoming the hospital's next CEO. One thing Nanette and Gary's easygoing love was showing her was that she was too good to settle for second best. Didn't she deserve to be with a man who loved her so wholly and completely? With a man who would cherish her for who she was?

Nanette's smile brightened naturally at Stacey's words and she nodded with eagerness. 'OK. Let me see my gorgeous husband.'

Stacey stayed with Nanette and Gary while the surgical registrar explained the operation, and after Gary had signed the consent form he was wheeled off to Theatres. Stacey took Nanette to the theatre patients' waiting room, where there was a tea and coffee machine, comfortable chairs and some up-to-date magazines to read.

She'd just settled Nanette with a cup of coffee when Pierce walked in.

'OK. Gary is heading into Theatre now. They'll perform a scan of his abdomen in there and then start the operation. They're just waiting on the report on the bloods, but for the moment everything is under control.'

Nanette sighed at this information and visibly relaxed. 'How much longer will things take? I mean, will he be able to come home later today?'

'No,' Stacey and Pierce answered in unison.

'He'll be in hospital for at least a few days,' Pierce added.

'Are you sure you want to stay and wait?' Stacey asked, putting a hand on Nanette's arm, concern in her tone. 'You could go home, get some rest, and we can call you when—'

'No.' Nanette cut off her words. 'I appreciate what you're saying but I'm staying right here. The kids are all sorted out with my neighbour, and I'm not going home to an empty house only to sit there and wait for my phone to ring.' She put her hand on Stacey's and gave it a little squeeze. 'You don't have to sit with me, Stacey. I know you need to get back to bed or see other patients or whatever else it is you doctors do during these crazy hours of the morning.'

'She *does* need to get home and get some more sleep. *I* may have the morning off, but poor Stacey here will have a plethora of housecalls to make once the sun comes up—and all without her trusty and faithful sidekick.'

Stacey's lips twitched at Pierce's words and she raised one eyebrow. 'Sidekick, eh?'

Nanette giggled, and it was good to see the other woman finding a small bit of lightness in her otherwise dark emotions.

'Absolutely. You're the superhero. I'm just your companion.'

'Companion?' Both eyebrows shot up this time and the smile increased.

'How about…assistant? Better word?'

Stacey shook her head slowly from side to side. 'How about none of the above? I don't want to be labelled a superhero. Too much pressure.'

Pierce spread his arms wide, as though she really were passing up a once-in-a-lifetime offer. 'Suit yourself.'

Nanette giggled again, then sighed—a long, relaxing type of sigh, indicating that a small part of her tension had been eased. 'Both of you go. I'll be more than fine here. I've got magazines to read—' She pointed to the small table. 'And free tea and coffee and these chairs,' She patted the armrest of the one she was seated in. 'Not too bad for a quick kip, and I have no children to bother me, so all in all a few pluses.'

'Now, *there's* a real superhero.' Pierce held out his hand to indicate Nanette.

The woman smiled and blushed a little beneath his gaze before literally shooing them both from the room.

'She's a nice lady,' Pierce commented as they headed back to the Emergency Department. 'How do you know her?'

'School. She was the year ahead of us.'

'And yet she knows you? I didn't think teenagers stepped outside their bonds of social hierarchy all that much.'

At the nurses' station Pierce sat down and picked up a pen, knowing he should probably stop chatting to Stacey and get back to the mound of case notes Sister had asked him to review. However, if it was a choice between paper-work and chatting with Stacey the decision was a no-brainer. Getting to know Stacey a lot better was presently top of his list of things to do.

'There wasn't too much hierarchy at our school. And besides, *everyone* knows us.' Stacey sat on the edge of the chair next to him and spread her hands wide. 'We're the Wilton triplets. Twins often get remarked upon, especially if they're identical, but triplets—let's just say we're used to being something of a novelty.'

'And do you have some psychic connection that lets you read each other's thoughts? I've heard that twins can have a bond like that. Surely it's greater in triplets?'

'I wouldn't call it a psychic connection, per se.' She thought for a moment, then shrugged. 'It's difficult to explain. I guess it's more like sharing an…emotion. I think it would be the same for any people who spend a lot of time together. The three of us have been together since birth, and I guess we…*feel* that essence of the emotion in each other.' She shook her head. 'It's so difficult to describe.'

'Like intuition?'

'Sort of but...*more* so.'

Pierce scratched his head, the corners of his mouth pulling upwards. 'You're right. You're not explaining it well.'

He tried not to chuckle when she snatched the pen from his hand and shook it at him.

'Listen, buddy. I've had very little sleep, so don't pick on me.'

Pierce couldn't stifle his laughter any longer, and the sound of his mirth warmed her through and through. What was it about him that constantly knocked her off balance, regardless of the time of day?

He held up his hands in surrender. 'Sorry. You're right, of course. Time you were off back home so you can get some rest.' He stood and told the duty sister that he'd be back soon. 'I'll walk you out to your car.'

'That's not necessary. You're needed here.'

'Not at the moment.' He indicated the eerily quiet Emergency Department. 'We're past the "danger hour", and apart from Gary the night hasn't been too bad. So...' Pierce crooked his elbow in her direction. 'If you will allow me, Dr

Wilton, I would be most pleased to escort you safely back to your car.'

Stacey looked around at the staff, wondering if they were all watching Pierce being a little bit silly but also incredibly charming, but most of them were too busy to notice. So as not to hurt his feelings, and feeling quite silly herself, whether due to lack of sleep, the release of tension from the past hour or so, or simply the fact that being around Pierce often made her feel delightfully free of restraint, Stacey curled her fingers around his elbow, resting her hand on his arm.

'Why, thank you, kind sir.'

He nodded politely in her direction before they headed off towards the doctors' car park, which was situated right next to the emergency parking bays where the ambulances arrived.

Neither of them spoke for a few minutes but Stacey didn't feel uncomfortable. The sky was cloudless, the stars were shining bright in the moonlight, but the breeze was quite chilly and she actually found herself snuggling a little closer to Pierce, drawn towards his natural body warmth.

'Cold?' he asked, and before she knew what was happening he'd manoeuvred their positions so that instead of offering her his arm in a gentlemanly manner he'd placed his firm, muscled arm about her, his hand resting at her waist, drawing her to him as they walked slowly along the path. 'Better,' he stated as he snuggled a little closer.

Stacey felt highly self-conscious at being embraced by him.

He breathed in and slowly exhaled. 'How can you smell so utterly delicious at such a time of the morning? Or perhaps,' he continued, 'you always smell this good.' He breathed in deeply again. 'Beautiful Stacey,' he whispered, and his sweet words caused goosebumps to flood her entire body.

When they reached her car Pierce gently turned to face her, leaning against the driver's door and bringing his other arm around her. She was now standing firmly in his embrace. Pierce was embracing her openly…here…in the doctors' car park. Granted it was almost four o'clock in the morning, and there was no one else around, but they were on display for all to see.

Stacey couldn't help glancing over her shoulder. She wasn't used to being demonstrative in public, especially because it had been one of the main things in her relationship with Robert that he'd been adamant would never happen. No public displays of emotion or affection. Pierce was so incredibly different…and she liked it a lot.

Pierce adjusted his legs, drawing her body closer to his. 'You *are* beautiful, Stacey. Do you know that?'

She lifted her hands to his chest, unsure whether she was trying to draw him close or keep him at bay. 'I…I'm…I don't know,' she replied, shaking her head as though she didn't believe a word he said.

'Well, *I* do.' Pierce looked down at her. 'Do you have any idea what you've done to me?'

'I'm sure I haven't *done* anything.'

He smiled. 'That's not what I meant, but when you say things like that, with your tone becoming all hesitant and awkward—well, it just makes it even more difficult for me to resist you.'

Stacey shook her head and closed her eyes, wanting him to stop saying things like that. Couldn't he see that they made her feel uncomfortable, that she wasn't used to receiving compliments?

'Why not?' he asked, gently brushing his fingers across her cheek, and it was only when he asked the question that she realised she'd spoken her thoughts out loud. 'What did that jerk of an ex-fiancé do to your self-esteem?' He cupped her cheek. 'Open your eyes, Stacey,' he commanded softly, and to her surprise, she found herself obeying. 'I don't care what any man may or may not have told you in the past, please believe me when *I* say that you are a beautiful, strong, intelligent woman and I would really like to get to know you better.' He raised his eyebrows.

She shook her head again. 'Pierce. Don't say things like—'

'I'm being honest here, Stacey,' he interrupted softly. 'I'm attracted to you and I want to spend some time with you, getting to know you.'

'We spend a lot of time together already.'

'Apart from at work,' he clarified. 'I'm happy to have your siblings around, if you feel as though you need a buffer, but I would also like to take you out on a date—just the two of us.' He was silent for about fifteen seconds, and the atmosphere between them became a little strained when Stacey didn't immediately respond. 'What do you think?' he prompted.

'Um…' She swallowed, her heart beating wildly against her chest. 'You're really serious about this? About this thing—?'

'Can't you feel it?' Pierce pressed her hand to his chest. 'My heart is pounding, Stace. It always does when you're nearby. I catch a glimpse of your smile as you talk to a patient and I'm swarmed with jealousy because I want you to smile at *me*. I hear you laugh on the phone when you're chatting with your sister and the sound relaxes me.'

'Really?'

'Yes, Stacey. Really.' There was intent in his words, as though he was desperate to make her believe he wasn't just feeding her a line. 'Other men may have put you down, may not have wanted to be seen in public with you— and, yes,' he continued before she could say a word, 'I'm aware of how you're self-conscious about showing even the slightest bit of affection in public. I want you to know that I'm not embarrassed or ashamed to be seen holding your hand, or putting my arms around you or…kissing you in public.'

As he spoke his gaze dropped to encompass her mouth. Her lips parted at his words, her heart-rate now completely out of control, every fibre in her being trembling with anticipatory delight. He sounded sincere. In fact he almost sounded slightly offended that she didn't believe him. But somehow he seemed to understand that things had been very different in her past relationships—especially with Robert.

It was nice to have him say these words to her, to reassure her. And yet she still felt as though something was holding her back…but what? Everything she'd seen of Pierce—his interaction with her family, his concern for Mike and Edna, his devotion to his sister—indicated that he was a good man and, as the old adage went, a good man was hard to find. Perhaps she should stop trying to fight him and instead accept that he was really interested in *her*. That he honestly did want to spend time with her simply because he liked her.

The realisation, the sensation of believing

Pierce was telling her the truth, made her heart fill with gladness.

'Do you want me to kiss you, Stacey?'

His words were barely a whisper, but they seemed so loud, echoing around her body in sync with the pounding of her heart.

'Yes.'

The single word escaped her lips before she could stop it. For a split second she thought Pierce hadn't heard her at all, but within the next moment his lips curved upwards with delight and his head began its slow descent.

'That, my gorgeous Stacey, is excellent news.'

And without further ado he captured her willing mouth with his own.

CHAPTER SEVEN

THE FEEL OF his lips on hers made her knees go weak and she slid her arms up and around his neck, clinging to him as he continued to bring her dormant senses to life. Robert had always maintained that kissing wasn't all that important in a relationship, that intellectual compatibility was far more necessary for a functioning and enduring life together. At the time Stacey had believed him, but now, with the way Pierce was filling her with light from the soft, sweet pressure of his touch, she knew she'd been oh-so wrong.

There was warmth in his touch, tenderness in the way he held her close. He'd called her beautiful and at the time she hadn't really believed him. But now, with the way he was pressing his lips to hers, taking his time, not wanting to rush a second of this unique and powerful experience,

Stacey was starting to believe he might have actually meant it.

Pierce thought she was beautiful! Accepting this filled her with a sense of wonder and confidence and she opened her mouth a little more, deepening the kiss, wanting to create some of the sensations she'd only dreamed about. He was here. This was real. And she was going to enjoy it.

Pierce's reaction was a deep, warm groan which signified his approval of the manoeuvre. She was delightful, delectable and utterly delicious. How was it possible he hadn't experienced such wonderment combined with innocence before? There was a freshness to her reaction, unstudied and raw, and with the way she was exerting control over the situation, showing him exactly what was contained beneath that quiet, calm exterior, he couldn't help but become even more enamoured with her.

The way her mouth opened to him, the way she responded to him—it was…*giving*. It was then that he truly accepted the fact that she'd always been a giver, always putting others before herself, offering to them the things they desired.

As he continued to savour the sweetness of her mouth he couldn't help the thread of confusion which passed through him. Stacey was giving him what he wanted, a heartfelt response, because giving to others was what she knew how to do.

Well, this time, he wanted her to *take*, to allow him to make her feel unique and special and cherished. Naturally, as they were standing in a car park, there was no way that things could progress now, but he had the sensation that where Stacey was concerned taking things nice and slow was definitely the way to go.

He eased back slightly, breaking his lips from hers, not surprised to find both of them breathing heavily from the sensations coursing through them. Good heavens, she was precious. Her eyelids were still closed, her face still angled towards his, her perfectly pink lips parted to allow pent-up air to escape.

Pierce marvelled in her beauty, and the need to explore her smooth, sweet skin was too much for him to resist. He brushed small butterfly kisses on her eyelids, delighted when she gasped in wonderment. Then he slowly made his way down her cheeks, tasting the freshness of her skin. The subtle scent of her perfume combined with the release of endorphins to provide a heady combination, and it was one he knew he could easily become addicted to.

With an all-encompassing tenderness she'd never felt before Pierce pressed kisses from her cheek around to her ear, where he lingered for a moment, causing her body to flood with a new mass of tingles. Then he worked his way down her neck and she found herself tipping her head to the side, granting him as much access as he wanted. He brushed her hair from her neck with the backs of his fingers, not wanting anything to hinder his exploration, his fingers trailing in the silky strands as though he couldn't get enough of the feel of her hair. How was it possible that such a simple action could fill her so completely with needs she'd never even known she had?

It wasn't until he kissed lower, brushing aside the top of her shirt collar, clearly intent on exploring further, that Stacey started to feel a sense of propriety return. She opened her eyes and tried to shift in his embrace, but Pierce spoke against her skin.

'It's all right, Stace.' he breathed. 'I'm not going to ravish you right here. I just want you to *feel.*'

'I do,' she whispered back. 'But…we're…out… in the open and…oh—' Her words were broken off as Pierce pressed kisses along her collarbone, clearly thrilled with her response to his touch as he made his way around to the other side.

'You are exquisite,' he murmured, taking his time, not wanting to rush the exploration.

Stacey tipped her head further back. Her eyes were open as she stared up at the stars, but the sensations he was evoking made it impossible for her to see clearly. It was evident that the attraction between them was incredibly powerful.

When he finally brought his mouth back to hers Stacey's hunger had intensified, and she opened her mouth wider than before, plunging her tongue into his mouth, wanting him to see exactly how he'd affected her senses, heightening them beyond belief. With a passion and urgency she'd never felt before she surrendered herself to him and to the emotions he evoked.

She threaded her fingers through his hair, making sure he didn't break away from her just yet, loving the feel of his arms firmly around her, encompassing her, making her feel secure as well as utterly sexy.

Was this how other people felt when they were kissed by someone who really desired them? Was this what she'd been missing out on? How was it possible she hadn't known that *this* was the way to kiss an attractive man? Or that this was the way a man kissed a woman he found attractive?

Feeling as though her lungs might completely burst if she didn't drag some oxygen into them, Stacey jerked her head back, needing to make a sharp clean break in order to breathe.

'Stacey...'

Her name was a caress upon his lips and she liked the way it sounded. She also liked that he was as breathless as her, as invested as her in all these new and crazy emotions.

'You really *do* like me.' Her words were an astonished whisper, filled with awe and happiness.

'Yes. Yes, I do,' he stated with a slight chuckle, and she immediately closed her eyes and buried her face in his chest.

'Sorry. Clearly I'm a little...knocked off balance by all of this. I keep blurting my thoughts out loud.'

'Is this a common occurrence?' he queried, dropping a kiss to her head, his fingers sifting through the silkiness of her hair.

'No. That's what's so confusing. Usually I'm quite in control of my faculties.' She eased back and looked up at him. 'But you...' She swallowed and smiled up at him. 'You make me feel alive.'

'That's a good thing, Stacey.'

'I know, but I'm clearly not used to it. Hence the unusual behaviour.'

'I'll let you in on a little secret,' he said, dipping his head closer to her ear. 'I like that you're a little unusual because that means you're unique.' He kissed her cheek.

She sighed and snuggled closer to him, wrapping her arms around him and resting her head against his chest, loving the words he was saying. Having been one of three all her life, it was refreshing to hear that he thought her unique.

The cool breeze, which he'd been oblivious to while he'd been memorising each and every contour of her face, whipped up around them, with a hint of saltiness from the sea not so far away.

'It's late…or rather early,' he murmured. 'And you need to get home.'

Stacey gasped. 'You're still on shift. How could we have forgotten?'

'If there'd been a problem they would have called.' He patted the cell phone in his trouser pocket. 'Besides, I haven't heard any sirens… except for you.' He chuckled and waggled his eyebrows at her.

'That's a very cheesy line,' she stated, smiling up at him and sighing once more.

'I thought you liked cheesy?'

'I do. I really do. But you're right. I'd best get home. House calls start in exactly…' She paused and squinted at her watch, unable to see the time. 'Some time soon.'

Pierce's warm laughter washed over her.

'Where are your keys?' he asked, releasing her from his embrace with obvious reluctance.

Stacey picked up her handbag, which had at some point slipped from her shoulder unnoticed to land at their feet. She dug around in the bag and eventually pulled them out.

'Amazing what you can find in a black hole,' he commented as she pressed the button to unlock her car. 'All women's handbags are black holes. I'm convinced of it. Even Nell's—although someone at work bought her an inner purse organiser which she absolutely loves. Still, it only means she can carry even *more* things around with her.'

Stacey chuckled as he opened the car door for her. He leaned forward and pressed another kiss to her lips. 'Drive safe.'

'OK. I hope the rest of your shift is uneventful.'

'You and me both. I'll give you a call when there's news of Gary.'

'Thanks. I'd appreciate that.' She smiled at him.

'And once we've discussed our mutual patient we can discuss exactly how we're going to spend the rest of our weekend—after you've finished the housecalls, of course.'

'We're going to spend our weekend together?'

'Why, yes, Stacey. That's what people do when they date. They spend time together.'

'Date?' The word squeaked from her lips and she stared at him with surprise.

Pierce chuckled once more, and was about to say something when his cell phone rang.

'Go. You're needed,' she told him.

He leaned forward and pressed a firm and secure kiss to her lips before extracting the phone from his pocket, then he winked at her and started jogging back towards the emergency department as he answered his call.

Stacey sat in the car and started the engine. 'We're *dating*?' She stated the words out loud as she buckled her seatbelt. '*I'm* dating?' She switched on the car's lights. 'Pierce and I are dating.' She tried to state the words with absolute firmness, as though it was the most natural thing in the world. 'This is good,' she remarked as she headed out of the car park and onto the road. 'Moving forward is good.'

Stacey seemed to float through the next week with a large smile plastered to her face. Her sister Molly was delighted at this turn of events.

'You're dating Pierce? *Really* dating? Really

putting yourself out there and doing something just for you?' Molly was gobsmacked.

'Yes.'

'And you're not overthinking things?'

'Nope. Just going with the flow.'

'Uh-huh.' Molly didn't sound as though she fully believed her, but she grinned wildly just the same.

When Stacey spoke to Cora over the internet chat line Cora knew something was different even before Molly blurted it out.

'You look really…happy, Stace,' she said, her tone laced with curiosity. 'What's going on over th—?'

'She's dating Pierce!' Molly squealed, jumping up and down and clapping her hands with utter delight.

From there, Stacey was plied with a barrage of questions from Cora—so much so that Cora demanded that the next time they were scheduled to talk Pierce should be there so she could 'meet' him.

'So I'm being served up for Cora's approval, eh?' Pierce said at the end of the week.

They'd just finished a hectic clinic day and

were relaxing in the kitchen with a soothing cup of herbal tea. Winifred had just left and the front door to the surgery was locked. It was just the two of them, and although she still felt highly self conscious about being alone with Pierce, Stacey was more than happy to have a bit of time with him.

They'd shared several meals together over the past week, with all of Stacey's siblings and Nell, too. George and Lydia had been demanding, craving adult male attention—especially when he spun them around in the back garden or gave them shoulder rides so they could pretend to be giraffes. And he was incredibly patient with them as they showed him the progress they'd made in training their rabbits in the art of professional rabbit jumping.

Nell enjoyed playing with the rabbits, and was getting good at making Andrew jump over obstacles. She still loved playing games, now openly including the other children, and liked to help in the kitchen when it was time for dinner. As setting the table was one of the things she did every night, she continued to do that job whenever she came to Stacey's house, and

George and Lydia were more than happy to hand over the task.

Jasmine was perhaps the one who had surprised them all the most, by insisting on taking over Nell's afternoon routine. 'You and Pierce work late. Nell needs someone right there for her when she gets off the bus. George is nine, so he can stay at home with Lydia—or they can come with me, too.'

'But she has an afternoon snack. You'd have to prepare that too,' Stacey had cautioned.

'Hello?' Jasmine had waved her two hands in front of Stacey's face. 'What are these? They're hands. I can prepare food with them. I'm not a little kid, you know.'

Stacey had talked this over with Pierce, who'd admitted that it *would* be good for someone to take over meeting Nell from the bus as sometimes he just wasn't able to get away from the clinic on time. And so Jasmine had taken over this responsibility and so far was doing exceptionally well.

Stacey had hoped that helping out Nell would stop Jasmine from being so surly with others, but it hadn't. And she'd stopped acknowledging Pierce's presence altogether.

'She's probably jealous,' Molly had said to her one night as they'd tried to figure out how they could handle the matter. Stacey had disciplined Jasmine, and given her consequences, but Jasmine simply didn't seem to care.

'Jealous? Of what?'

'Of Pierce. She probably thinks you've got less time for her now.'

'Has she said something?'

Molly had shaken her head. 'Not to me. I'm just spit-balling ideas here.'

Stacey had closed her eyes and shaken her own head. 'How do we reach her, Molly? What do we need to do to let her know we're on her side?'

Molly's phone had rung and she'd quickly pulled it from her pocket. 'Sorry, Stace. I'm second on call.'

'Sure.'

Stacey had waved Molly's words away and within another ten minutes her sister had gone, heading towards the hospital to assist with the patients involved in multiple car crash on the M1. As this was the main road from Sydney to

Newcastle, Stacey had had no idea when Molly might return to finish their conversation. Once again she'd been left holding the ball, needing to make most of the decisions and carry out the majority of discipline.

Stacey wanted to talk to Pierce about it—see if he had any ideas—but it wasn't his problem. Besides, if she did speak to Pierce about her younger sister and Jasmine found out she might stop going to see Nell, not wanting anything to do with Pierce or his sister. That risk was too great, so Stacey was left to try and figure it out on her own.

'Do you think Cora will like me?' Pierce asked, bringing her thoughts back to the present.

Stacey smiled as she placed her arms around his shoulders, delighted that she was allowed to touch him in such a familiar way. 'I have no doubt about it.'

'Excellent. Then that leaves only Jasmine.'

'Jasmine doesn't like *anyone*, Pierce, so don't take it personally. I'm trying not to.'

'She's nice to Nell, for which I am very grateful,' he remarked. He thought for a moment, then said, 'How about a picnic next weekend?'

Stacey considered it. 'The weather's supposed to be nice. King Edward Park?'

'Perfect.' He kissed her a few more times. 'Just like your mouth. Perfect for mine.'

She smiled and sighed into his embrace, more than happy for him to take his time exploring the contours of her 'perfect' mouth. Pierce was always saying such lovely things to her—telling her she had luscious hair and that he loved running his fingers through it, or that she was beautiful, precious and deserved to be loved not only for the pureness of her heart but also because of the sadness in her eyes.

'I'm not sad,' she'd replied after Pierce had whispered the compliment near her ear the other evening when he'd been kissing her goodnight.

Pierce had brushed her loose hair behind her ears and kissed both of her cheeks. 'I'm getting to know you better, Stacey and I can't believe the weight you have to carry on those slim shoulders of yours.'

He'd placed his large warm hands onto her shoulders as he'd spoken, massaging gently, releasing endorphins that had made her want to melt into his arms for ever and never leave.

'I care about you, Stacey. More and more every day. But the sadness which you've buried deep down inside is dangerous.'

'Dangerous?' She'd tried to laugh off his words, but the sound had been hollow even to her own ears.

'If we're not careful sadness can consume us.'

'You sound as though you know what you're talking about.' She'd eased back from his massaging hands and he'd instantly stopped the motion.

'I do.'

'Grief over your parents' loss?'

'Yes. The death of a loved one can leave such a wide and gaping chasm, and if we're not careful—if we don't take the time to heal the wound from the inside out but just keep changing the dressing and applying a new bandage to the wound—then infection can set in.'

He'd brushed the back of his fingers across her cheek before pulling her closer into his arms. They'd stood there for a while, with Stacey revelling in the feel of his arms wound tightly around her, before he'd finally spoken again.

'I understand the brokenness, the pain, the desolation that grief can bring, whatever the circumstances which have caused it. Along with all of these comes loneliness, and whilst I know you have a very supportive family, and you seem more than willing and able to shoulder the lion's share of that responsibility, at times you seem so lonely.'

'Lonely?' She'd eased back slightly and looked up at him. 'I've never been alone in my life. I'm one of three. I wasn't even alone in the womb! And let's not forget I have five siblings.'

'And yet sometimes…' He'd exhaled slowly, his words filled with understanding. 'You're so lonely. I just wanted you to know that I've been there, too.' He'd bent his head and brushed his lips across hers. 'The weight of your world is not yours alone to carry. Please let me help you in any way I can.'

His words had held promise, his touch had held promise, even the taste of his lips on hers had held promise…so why was she having such a difficult time letting go of the chains that bound her? Had she been carrying the responsibility for her family for far longer than she'd realised?

When her father had married Letisha, when

they'd had Jasmine, hadn't it been Stacey who had helped the most, wanting to do everything she could to make things easier for her step-mother? Cora and Molly had been delighted with their new sibling, and indeed, when George and Lydia had rounded out their family, the triplets had loved having younger sisters and a brother to entertain. But whenever they'd been asked to babysit it had been Stacey who had taken charge.

Have I always done this? she asked herself later that night. Now that he'd pointed out the wound Stacey had thought already healed, especially since returning to Newcastle to connect to her roots, she was more than aware of the way both Molly and Cora really did leave it up to her to call the shots.

She wanted to talk to Molly about it, but her poor sister had been rostered on with such long shifts that as soon as she arrived home she'd quickly eat something before collapsing into such a deep sleep Stacey hadn't the heart to wake her.

She loved her siblings—all of them—and would do anything for any of them. They'd do the same for her...wouldn't they?

She tried not to fixate on the question as she went about her daily life, happy that George and Lydia were settling into school but with increasing concern for Jasmine's declining behaviour.

Indeed, when she informed everyone they would be having a picnic in the park the following weekend they'd all been excited except for Jasmine. Even the information that Nell was looking forward to seeing her there hadn't changed Jasmine's attitude.

'I have no idea what to do,' Stacey confessed to Cora during one of their internet chats. 'She really seems to hate me.'

'That's because you're the disciplinarian.'

'How did I get *that* job?'

Cora laughed. 'I don't know. I guess as you're the oldest triplet we've always just naturally looked up to you. At school whenever there was a problem you always came up with a solution. Some people are born leaders, Stace, and you're one of them. Just look at how you've held us all together over the past eighteen months. And when you decided to buy Dad's old practice Molly and I gave our blessing because we trust your judgement. We knew you would have figured all the angles, weighed up the pros and cons.'

'And yet I've hurt Jasmine the most by uprooting her from her friends.'

'The practice would have closed down if you hadn't bought it when you did. It's necessary for that community to have a functioning, working medical practice and you've put the needs of the many ahead of the needs of a fourteen-year-old girl who will one day forgive you.'

'Will she?'

'Did you forgive Dad when he followed his dreams and took us all to Perth?'

'Yes, but—'

'You followed your dreams, Stacey. You did what you knew was right deep down in your heart. Jasmine isn't collateral damage. Far from it. Just look at how she's helping more with George and Lydia, how she's helping Pierce's sister. Those are *good* things.'

Stacey sighed. 'I guess.'

'You've held us all together for so long—plus you've had your own personal emotional dramas to contend with. And although Molly and I are always there for you—and we know you know this—you still need those moments of solitude.'

'But I don't *want* solitude.'

'Don't you?' Cora was surprised. 'I always thought that sometimes, with the three of us living in each other's pockets all our lives, you just needed some space to breathe.'

'Do you?'

Cora thought on this for a moment. 'I think I find my solitude in adventure.' She spread her arms wide, indicating the military-style truck behind her. 'Just to speak to you like this I have to borrow a truck, drive an hour through rough, dirty tracks that any ordinary four-wheel drive would get stuck in, and then head to the top of a mountain where the satellite transmission is strongest.'

'And I appreciate every time you've done this. I know it must cut into your valuable work there in Tarparnii.'

'But you see, Stace, that's my point. I *like* going four-wheel driving—just like Molly loves dancing and going on clown patrol and joining in with every social activity any hospital runs. That's *her* solitude. Yours is to contemplate the meaning of life.' Cora smiled at her sister. 'And I know Jazzy's causing you concern, but perhaps she's just trying to find her own place—her thing she likes the most.'

'Her solitude?'

'Her happy place,' Cora offered.

Stacey sighed. 'I hope she finds it soon.'

'What about you?'

'What *about* me?'

'Have you found *your* happy place?'

'What do you mean?'

'You're different, Stace.'

'I am?'

'Yes.' Cora threw her arms in the air. 'Can't you see it? Feel it?'

'Feel…what?'

'Pierce! Stacey, I'm talking about *Pierce*. Even over the internet chat I could see he was dreamy. You've picked a winner there.'

Stacey's smile widened as she tucked her hair behind her ear. 'Oh, Cora. He makes me feel so…tingly and shiny and…and…'

'Happy?'

'Yes. That's why I guess I've been feeling

guilty about Jasmine—because for the first time in a long time I'm…happy.'

'Don't feel guilty, Stace. Accept it. Draw strength from the way Pierce makes you feel. You deserve a world of happiness—especially after you-know-who.'

'It's OK,' Stacey replied. 'You can say his name now, because with the way Pierce makes me feel I've realised that whatever it was I had with Robert it certainly wasn't love.'

'Wait. wait, wait!' Cora clasped her hands together and stared at her sister. 'What are you saying? Are you saying that you're *in love* with Pierce?'

Stacey's smile was bright and wide and filled with delight. 'I…I…think so.'

Cora squealed with excitement. 'Oh, Stace, really? This is wonderful, great—and a whole heap of other awesome adjectives.'

Stacey laughed, loving her sister and wishing she was there in person so they could hug.

'Say it again,' Cora demanded, clapping her hands.

'I think I might be in love with Pierce Brolin,' Stacey stated, and even as she said the words out loud she knew that it was far more absolute than she was willing to admit even to her sister.

She didn't just *think* she was in love with Pierce. She *knew* it with all her heart… But for now, although she adored her sisters and the close bond they shared, she needed to keep that intimate piece of information to herself.

CHAPTER EIGHT

'I SEE YOU and Stacey are spending a bit more time together,' Mike said as he tossed some poker chips into the middle of the table. Edna had already lost all her chips and gone off to make them a cup of tea.

'Yes.' Pierce had been wondering when Mike might bring up the topic of Stacey. 'I see your chips and I raise you.'

Their friendly poker games had been going on throughout Mike's recovery which, Pierce had to admit, was good. Mike was adhering to the diet his cardiologist had recommended and was also looking forward to the rabbit jumping competition George and Lydia were planning to attend.

Mike considered his cards, then tossed the same amount of chips into the centre of the table. 'Call. What have you got?'

For a moment Pierce wasn't sure whether Mike was talking about the cards or about the fact that he'd been spending more time with Stacey. Mike was very protective of all the Wilton children, taking on the role of family patriarch with pride.

'I have got a full house,' Pierce remarked, placing his cards on the table.

Mike chuckled and didn't cough once, which Pierce was pleased to note.

'That you do, boy. If you're serious about Stacey there'll definitely be a full house. Are you up to taking on that level of responsibility again? Raising siblings?' Mike placed one hand over the pile of chips in the centre of the table.

Pierce had thought about it—especially as he was spending more and more time not only with Stacey but with the rest of her siblings. She was a package deal. He couldn't have one without the other. He was the same. He would always have Nell in his life. But she was now at the stage where one of her housemates, Samantha, had moved in, and the event they'd meticulously planned and structured for many years could now finally take place: Nell living independently.

But Stacey...beautiful, wonderful Stacey. She responded to his kisses as though she'd never been kissed before, as though she'd never felt this way before, and, he'd had to admit he felt a connection with Stacey that he hadn't felt with any other woman before.

'Well?' Mike brought Pierce's thoughts back to the present.

Pierce looked down at the cards neatly laid in a row. Full house. Was he ready?

'I wanted to find out whether this thing between Stacey and myself was something special—whether it was worth pursing.'

'And is it?'

Pierce reached out, lifted Mike's hand from the pile and pulled all the chips towards him. 'Yes.'

Mike gaped. 'But what about the job? The one they're constantly bugging you to come over for?'

Pierce shrugged. 'Some dreams aren't meant to come true. I learned that lesson a long time ago.'

'Hmm...' Mike looked at his friend. 'I hope you're right.'

Pierce nodded. 'Stacey's worth it.'

'Your feelings are that strong?'

He thought about Mike's question for a moment. *Were* they that strong? *Was* Stacey worth sacrificing his main chance to head over to Yale and lead a team of researchers? He'd been wanting to do that for so long now, but Nell had always come first and there had been no way he was going to choose a job over his most beloved sister. Now Nell was settled and he was free to go, to follow his dream—the one he'd been aiming towards for such a very long time.

And yet there was the way Stacey was able to see into his heart, to understand everything he'd already sacrificed for the love of a sibling, and the way she felt in his arms—as though he'd finally found *his* home, the place where *he* belonged… Were his feelings strong enough that he would never have regrets at turning down the only job he'd ever really wanted?

Pierce's answer was a firm nod in the affirmative, yet for some reason he couldn't bring himself to speak the word *yes* out loud once more. But he was certain he was falling in love with Stacey, and he was prepared to love and accept not only her but the rest of her family, just as she loved and accepted Nell.

'I hope you're right, boy,' Mike remarked as

he shuffled the deck of cards. 'Ready for another hand?'

Pierce eyed his huge pile of chips, then looked at Mike and smiled. 'Sure. What have I got to lose?'

Mike's answer was a wise old chuckle. 'If you're not careful? Everything.'

The following Saturday the sun was shining brightly, making the early October day perfect for a picnic in the park. Unfortunately, by the time they all arrived at King Edward Park, it had become clear that several other people had had the same idea, and all the council-provided barbecues were already in use.

'We'll have to queue for the barbecue,' joked Samantha, Nell's new housemate, as they spread picnic blankets beneath a large shady gum tree. Nell was already getting excited and pulling a Frisbee out of the bag she'd brought with her.

'Come on, Jasmine,' she ordered, reaching for Jasmine's hand and tugging the surly teenager along. 'Come and play Frisbee with me.'

Jasmine did as she was bid, not looking at anyone but not grumbling about it either.

'Jasmine's still not happy?' Pierce asked, placing a supportive arm around Stacey's shoulders.

'Cora says she's searching for her happy place.'

'Perhaps Cora's right. I think everyone searches for their happy place.'

They stood there for a moment, watching Jasmine let Nell boss her around. Stacey wondered whether there was something more to Pierce's words. Had he found *his* happy place? Was he happy? With her?

'She's incredibly good with Nell,' he continued, and Stacey detected no unhappiness in his voice so allowed herself to relax into his embrace.

He put his other arm around her, enfolding her against him. She closed her eyes, allowing herself to breathe in his strength, to breathe in the feel of his supporting arms around her. She'd never understood before how others could draw strength just from receiving a hug from someone else—not until she'd met Pierce. But when he hugged her like this she *did* draw strength from him, and for the first time since they'd moved to Newcastle she saw a glimmer of hope that everything would turn out all right.

'Are you two going to cuddle and kiss *all* day long?' Lydia demanded, wrapping her arms around Stacey's waist.

Pierce instantly broke the contact and bent to scoop Lydia up, then placed his free arm over Stacey's shoulder, bringing Lydia into their hug.

'What's wrong with that?' Pierce asked as he kissed Lydia's cheek. The little girl wrapped her arms about his neck and snuggled into him.

'You smell nice,' she told him.

Pierce sniffed her hair. 'So do you.'

Lydia giggled. 'That's 'cause I've got Stacey's perfume on.'

'Ah…is that what it is?' Pierce sniffed Stacey, then Lydia, and nodded his head. 'Yep. Two gorgeous girls…perfectly ripe for…*tickling*!'

And with that he tickled Stacey's neck before doing the same to Lydia. The little girl let forth a peal of laughter and Stacey chuckled, her heart delighting at the way Pierce seemed to fit so perfectly with her family.

Although Molly had been called to an emergency a few hours ago she had hopes of joining them later. But with almost all of the people she loved the most nearby Stacey really did feel as though *this* was her happy place. *Her* family—complete with Nell and Pierce.

It was as though she hadn't realised there were pieces of her life missing—not until she'd met this man and his sweet sister. She was still constantly delighting in the sensations and emotions spending time with Pierce evoked, but in the back of her mind there were questions. Questions about what the future might hold and where this relationship was going. About what Pierce really wanted from his life. Was he willing to take on her ready-made family? Or did the thought put him off, as it had Robert?

Pierce had told her about the research team—the ones he wrote his articles for. And he'd told her they'd offered him a job—the same job—several times over. Now that Nell was settled and beginning to live her life of independence was Pierce going to head overseas? To lead the team of researchers? Or did he plan to stay here?

The turmoil of her thoughts kept her awake at night. Her life had been affected by indecision, questions and trauma, and it had made her the sort of person who needed to know where she was going, to map out a path of what the future might hold. If she could deal in absolutes then so much the better, but she had also had to learn how to adapt when life threw her curve balls.

'I *said*...' George remarked, tapping her on the arm. 'When are we going to cook? I'm hungry.'

Stacey snapped out of her reverie and looked at her brother. 'Your default setting is "I'm hungry".' She ruffled his hair and smiled. 'There are bananas and apples in the picnic basket. Have one of those to tide you over.'

She glanced at the rectangular brick barbecues provided by the council for everyone to use. All of them were still being used. She glanced over to where a new family was arriving at the park, looking around to stake out their piece of shady grass. The dad carried a portable barbecue and a gas bottle.

'We should have brought our own barbecue, too,' George grumbled, pointing to the family who'd thought ahead.

'Possibly,' Pierce agreed, 'but the point of coming to the park isn't just to eat a barbecued sausage, George.'

'It isn't?'

Pierce laughed. 'Come on. I think there's a football in the bag. Let's go kick it around.'

'Can I come, too?' Lydia asked.

'Yeah, Lydia's really good at football,' George agreed, his grumbling stomach momentarily forgotten as he raced over to the bag Pierce had pointed to. Pierce released a squirming Lydia from his arms and she ran off after her brother.

'They really don't stand still at that age, do they?' Pierce commented as he leaned over and pressed a contented kiss to Stacey's waiting lips.

'You're thirty-six and *you* don't stand still,' she pointed out with a chuckle.

'You're probably right,' he agreed, kissing her again before winking and jogging off to join George and Lydia on a free patch of grass.

Stacey sat down on the blanket next to Samantha, who was more than happy to sit quietly and absorb the atmosphere. Stacey watched as the family who'd brought their own barbecue hooked up the gas cylinder and began to cook their food. A few of the other barbecues were now being vacated, but at the moment she was in no hurry to rush over there and claim one. Pierce was right. Today wasn't just about barbecuing food but about spending time together, in the sunshine, enjoying each other's company.

She slipped on her sunglasses, watching as Jasmine threw the Frisbee at Nell, who didn't manage to catch it and had to run after it. Jasmine laughed and the sound washed over Stacey like manna from heaven. For this moment in time her little sister was happy. Perhaps that was enough for now.

Stacey closed her eyes, filled with a quiet contentment.

A loud scream jolted her eyes open and she pulled off her sunglasses, her heart pounding wildly.

'What?' She blinked a few times and in the next instant a loud whooshing noise seemed to surround the area, shaking every fibre of her being.

'Stacey!' She heard her name being called and scrambled to her feet. Samantha, too, was on her feet, staring, aghast, at what was happening. Panic seemed to engulf the entire park, with some people screaming, others running, and some, like her, standing and staring, trying to take everything in at a glance.

'What do I do? What do I do?' Samantha's high-functioning Asperger's was starting to show itself.

Stacey's mind clicked into doctor mode and she handed Samantha a set of car keys. 'Go to my car and get the big emergency bag from the boot. It's a big red backpack with a white cross on it.'

'OK. OK.' Glad of something to do, Samantha started to focus, and she quickly took the keys from Stacey and did as she was asked.

Stacey stood on the picnic rug and gazed out at the scene. The world seemed to pause as she took in her surroundings, her quick mind piecing together exactly what had happened.

Pierce, Lydia and George were all standing together. Pierce had grabbed their hands, ready to lead them from any danger. Jasmine was standing further away, her hands covering her open mouth, her eyes staring off into the distance in complete shock.

Stacey followed the line of Jasmine's gaze, her own eyes opening wide as she realised why her sister looked so distraught. Nell lay sprawled on the ground, the Frisbee nearby. Nell wasn't moving.

All of this registered in Stacey's mind within one glance.

The next thing to register was the cloud of black smoke filling the air, caused by a flaming ball of gas. The man and woman who had been cooking on the portable barbecue had been thrown to the ground as well, the man writhing and yelling in pain.

'Gas fire!'

Pierce's words broke through Stacey's haze, speeding her thoughts back to normal. He was walking quickly towards her, dodging people as they ran past him. Panic was beginning to grip the entire park. He was still holding onto George and Lydia's hands.

'There must have been a damaged regulator or hose and a fat fire has ignited it,' he called to her.

When they reached the rug George wrapped his arms around Stacey's waist and Lydia just stood and stared. Stacey pointed to where Nell lay on the ground.

'Pierce! Look!'

She watched as he turned, his expression

changing from one of controlled concern to one of complete despair as he took in the vision of his beloved little sister lying still on the grass.

'Go!' she urged when he stood still for a split second, his world clearly falling apart. 'Check her. I'll bring the medical kit over.'

'Uh…' Pierce nodded as though his mind was unable to compute which action he should take next. 'Yeah…yeah.' With that he all but sprinted over to where his sister lay.

Stacey turned her attention to her siblings. 'George, Lydia.' She bent down to hug them both, her words fast and stern. 'I need you to stay right here. *Right here.*' She pointed to their rug, which was on the opposite side of the park from where the explosion had occurred.

People were beginning to gather their belongings and leave, others were on their cellphones, hopefully calling the emergency services, others were taking photographs. There was a hive of activity, but the first thing Stacey had to do was to make sure her brother and sister were out of harm's way. Their safety was paramount.

'Wait for Samantha to get back from the car and then do exactly as she says.'

'Yes, Stacey,' they both answered, their little eyes wide with fear.

People were everywhere, and when Samantha came rushing back with the large emergency kit, Stacey nodded her thanks.

'Can you stay with the kids, please?'

Before Samantha could answer, Stacey took the backpack and raced over towards the man who was still screaming, writhing around on the grass. She could smell burning clothes and flesh. Whilst only seconds had passed since the explosion it felt a lot longer, with her mind trying to process too many things at once. For now, though, Pierce was attending to Nell, and although Stacey wanted nothing more than to check Nell herself, she had to prioritise.

The initial fireball which had scared them all was still burning, but thankfully the man hadn't put the portable barbecue beneath any trees, so although it was extremely hot the flames were now shooting upwards rather than billowing outwards. The man had stopped rolling and she realised he was no longer on fire, but his body might be going into shock or worse.

She knelt down beside him, placing the emergency kit nearby. She called to her patient but received no response. She pressed two fingers to his radial pulse, relieved when she felt it—faint, but there. She was fairly sure he hadn't sustained any spinal damage, especially with the way he'd been rolling on the grass before losing consciousness. She opened her kit and quickly pulled on some gloves before finding a soft neck brace to help secure the man's spine, knowing that paramedics would replace it with a more rigid one. She called to the man again, telling him what she was doing, but he remained unconscious.

'Are you a medic?' she heard a woman ask.

'Yes.' Stacey glanced up for a moment.

'Good. I'm a volunteer firefighter.'

'Excellent.' Stacey inclined her head towards the blaze. 'You OK to deal with that?'

'My friends and I are. All the emergency services have been called. My friend's just getting an extinguisher from my car.'

'Great. Thanks.'

True to her word, the firefighter and her friends concentrated on dealing with the blaze, keeping it contained. Less than five minutes had passed

since the initial eruption, and even as she concentrated on her patient Stacey could also hear
several other people taking charge, marshalling
families together and generally controlling the
situation. It was good, because it made it far
easier for her to concentrate.

Nell wasn't lying too far away and she could
hear Pierce speaking to her and Nell talking
back. Stacey breathed an inward sigh of relief
to know that Nell was OK.

'You're all right,' she heard Pierce say. 'You've
just hurt your ankle, so I want you to stay as still
as possible. I'm going to get some bandages from
Stacey's medical kit and take care of it.'

Stacey glanced over and saw Pierce kiss his
sister's forehead before looking over his shoulder at her. Their gazes held for a brief second
and she could see the relief in his eyes. His sister was going to be all right.

Stacey was also aware of Jasmine in the back-
ground behind Pierce. She was still standing in
the same spot, hands still across her mouth, as
though she were unable to move or think, hor-
ror reflected in her eyes. Stacey wanted nothing more than to put her arms around her, to tell

her that everything would be OK, to comfort her when she needed it most, but instead Stacey called again to her patient, still receiving no response.

'Trev? Trev?' A woman crawled along the grass, coming towards Stacey. 'Trev! Get away from him!' she demanded, her words slurred, her eyes narrowed and filled with all the protectiveness of a possessive lioness.

'I'm a doctor,' Stacey told her. 'His name is Trev?'

'Yes.' The woman's attitude changed to one of hope as she came closer, reaching out to touch his head. 'What's wrong with him? Why isn't he moving?'

'I want to find out, but I need you to stay back. Give him some room.' Stacey kept her tone firm and direct. She mentally ran through what needed to happen next: do Trev's obs and assess the severity of his burns.

Thankfully, due to the volunteer firefighters, the blaze was now almost under control.

As she looked down at Trev, Stacey knew she was going to need further assistance. 'Pierce. I need you,' she called, glancing over at him before checking Trev's airway was clear.

'Acknowledged. I've just finished Nell's bandage.' Pierce wrapped Nell in a big hug and whispered something in her ear before he looked over and called to Jasmine, who was still rooted to the spot, unable to move. 'Jasmine? Can you come and help Nell, please?'

Jasmine shook her head from side to side before turning and running away.

'Jasmine! *Jasmine!*' he called, but the teenager wasn't listening. Pierce looked across at Stacey, unsure what to do.

Stacey stared wide-eyed at her sister's retreating back. There was nothing she could do. She couldn't go after Jasmine, which was her initial instinct. She needed to stay with her patient. She just had to trust that Jasmine's common sense would kick in at some point and she wouldn't stray too far from where they all were.

'I'll have to deal with her later.' The words were like dust in her mouth and her heart broke that she couldn't be there for Jasmine when she needed her most. 'Get Nell over to the rug with the others. Samantha, George and Lydia can look after her,' Stacey called, knowing she needed to focus completely on Trev rather than having her attention diverted by other personal matters.

'Right.' Pierce stood and scooped Nell up into his arms, carrying her over to the rug, where George and Lydia instantly rallied around her. Poor Samantha was doing her best to try and marshal some of the other children together—especially the two boys who had been kicking the football around with Pierce and were now quite distraught about their father—the man called Trev.

'I want to see my mum!' one of them yelled.

'What's wrong with my dad?' the other one questioned.

Stacey closed her eyes for a split second, focusing her thoughts on Trev and Trev alone. When she opened her eyes Pierce was coming round to Trev's other side.

'Status?' He pulled on a pair of gloves and reached for the stethoscope.

'Airway clear. Burns to hands, arms, both legs, and minor damage to the face. No response to calls. Trev?' she called again as she reached into the emergency medical kit to find a bag of saline and a package of IV tubing. 'We'll replenish fluids to avoid the possible complication of shock.'

'I love that you have such a well-stocked emergency kit,' Pierce commented as he unhooked the stethoscope. 'Heart-rate is mildly tachy. Pain meds?'

'Suggest ten milligrams of IV morphine followed by methoxyflurane.' Stacey's hands were busy, opening the packets of tubing and then looking for the best place to insert the line.

'Agreed. Allergies?'

Stacey looked over to where Trev's wife was sitting, rocking back and forth. Someone had had the presence of mind to wrap a blanket around her. 'Is Trev allergic to anything?' Stacey asked.

'Left arm isn't as badly damaged as the right arm,' Pierce commented as he assisted Stacey with setting up the drip.

She looked over to where the volunteer firefighter was standing back. The fire situation was now under control, the gas in the bottle having almost expired.

'Can you help?' Stacey called the woman over, indicating the saline bag, which would need to be held.

The woman nodded and made her way to Stacey, pleased to be of further assistance.

'Is Trev allergic to anything?' Pierce asked Trev's wife the question again, sharing a brief concerned look with Stacey.

The woman was clearly shocked at what had happened but hopefully wouldn't go into shock completely. The right side of her face was starting to droop, which might indicate nerve damage. First, though, they needed to stabilise Trev as best they could.

'Uh… Um…allergies? Um…I don't know. Is he going to be all right?'

'Does he take any regular medication? Has he had any alcohol today?'

'He's had two light beers and…uh…he takes… um…fish oil tablets. The doctor said his cholesterol is high.'

'Has he had any operations? Been hospitalised?' Pierce asked.

'No. No. He…uh…no.'

Stacey nodded and pulled out a pre-drawn syringe labelled 'morphine'. 'Check ten milligrams,' she stated.

'Check,' Pierce replied, and as soon as the saline drip was working Stacey administered the medication while Pierce told the still unconscious Trev what they were doing.

'Is that going to help him?' his wife wanted to know, watching everything they did with eyes as wide as saucers.

'It's going to relieve his pain,' Stacey offered, before they set to work on carefully bandaging the worst of Trev's leg wounds. She was ecstatic when the faint sounds of sirens could be heard in the distance. Whether police, fire brigade or ambulance, she didn't care—at least help was on the way.

Pierce took Trev's pulse again. 'A definite improvement.'

'And just in time to be transferred to an ambulance. Trev, help is here,' she told him as Pierce continued to perform neurological observations.

Stacey had just finished applying the last bandage when the paramedics came racing over. Pierce gave them a debrief while Stacey pulled off one set of gloves and pulled on another, moving quickly over to where Trev's wife sat, still staring at her husband.

'What's your name?' Stacey asked as she checked the side of the woman's face.

'Rowena.'

The word was barely a whisper, and the side of her mouth was drooping down. Stacey reached for a penlight torch and checked the woman's pupils, relieved when both responded to light.

'What are they doing to Trev?' Rowena asked, trying to look around Stacey, who was blocking her view.

'They're transferring him to a stretcher so they can get him into the ambulance. Just sit still for me a moment, Rowena.' Stacey spoke calmly but with a firmness that made Rowena look at her. Stacey pressed gloved fingers gently to Rowena's face, looking carefully.

'What is it? What's wrong?' she asked.

Stacey lifted the blanket off Rowena's shoulders and checked her right arm and side, realising there were several cuts and abrasions down the left side of Rowena's body. 'Rowena? What happened when the fire started? Do you remember?'

'Uh…' She looked at Stacey with scared eyes. 'What is it? Just tell me.'

'The left side of your face is drooping. That's why you're slurring your words.'

'I'm slurring?'

Rowena immediately went to lift a hand to touch her face, but Stacey stilled her arm and Rowena winced. Stacey immediately felt her ribs, gently checking to see if any of them were broken.

'Does it hurt when you breathe in?'

Rowena tried for a deep breath and immediately winced in pain. 'What *is* it? What's *wrong* with me?' The paramedics were securing Trev to the stretcher and Rowena's gaze followed her husband's supine form. 'Oh, why did this happen? *Why?*'

'Can you remember what did happen?' Stacey prompted again.

'I heard Trev yelling and I looked over and it was as though he was on fire—but only for a moment, and then he just dropped and…and… started rolling and yelling and…and…he was moving at an odd angle and it was all blurry and then I crawled over and you told me to get back.'

'Do you remember falling down?'

Stacey also thought back to that moment when

the world around her had seemed to slow down. Where had Rowena been? Stacey looked over to where two folding chairs were still on the ground, unpacked. They were the new kind of folding chair, with firm metal rods for stabilisation. Had Rowena landed on the folded-up chairs? Had she stumbled or been thrown backwards slightly, and ended up breaking a rib and possibly damaging a nerve in her face? Stacey could definitely remember seeing her lying down, so the scenario wasn't completely absurd.

Trev was now securely strapped to the stretcher, his neck in a firm neck brace, an IV pole holding the saline drip up high, releasing life-giving fluid to a patient who still hadn't regained consciousness.

'Where are they taking him? I want to go with him,' Rowena stated.

'I need to finish checking you over,' Stacey told her as she took Rowena's pulse, knowing the woman's elevated reading might well be due to the fact that she was highly concerned about her husband.

'But I can walk. I can move. I can stand.' As

though to prove it, Rowena tried to get to her feet but instantly wobbled.

Stacey put out a hand to steady her. 'Perhaps just stay still for a moment and let us get organised.' Stacey beckoned to one of the paramedics, who instantly came over, his own emergency medical kit on his back. 'This is Rowena,' she told the paramedic, whose green jumpsuit declared his surname was Wantanebe. 'Suspected L3 L4 fracture, possible damaged facial nerve. Neck brace, Penthrane green whistle, then stabilise and stretcher.'

'Yes, Doctor.'

'Pass me a stethoscope, please?' She held out her hand and had the instrument immediately provided for her.

She was listening to Rowena's breathing when Pierce came over, Trev now being secure in the ambulance.

'How are things going?' he asked as he knelt down beside Stacey, the stethoscope from her own kit still slung around his neck.

'Breathing is a little raspy on the left due to possible rib fracture.'

'How's my Trev?' Rowena asked anxiously.

Pierce smiled warmly at her. 'I'm pleased to announce he regained consciousness a moment after we'd secured him in the ambulance.'

This news definitely seemed to calm Rowena down. 'That's good, right? That's good, yeah?'

'It *is* good news,' Pierce confirmed as he pulled on a fresh pair of gloves and reached for a bandage. 'Let's get you stabilised and into the other ambulance. Is there someone who can come and be with your boys?' he asked.

It was only then that Rowena even seemed to remember her children, and Stacey was thankful the paramedic had already secured a neck brace in place, otherwise Rowena might have done some damage with the way she tried to whip her head around.

'Jeremiah and Lucas? Where are they? Oh, how could I have forgotten them?'

'They're fine.' Stacey needed to calm Rowena immediately. 'Our friend Samantha is looking after them. Just over there. On the rug under the big eucalyptus.'

She pointed to where Samantha seemed to be surrounded by several children, including Rowena's boys, George and Lydia, Nell, and thankfully Jasmine, too. Stacey wasn't sure when her sister had returned to the rug but she was relieved to see her there.

'They're all right? They didn't get hurt?'

'They're both fine. Do you want them to come in the ambulance with you?'

'Yes, and I'll…I'll call my neighbour to come and get them from the hospital.'

'That sounds like a wonderful plan,' Pierce told her, his deep voice sounding like a comfortable blanket.

Rowena seemed more capable of relaxing now, and even managed a small lopsided smile in his direction. What was it about this man that seemed to cause women to relax and melt? Was it the sound of his rich baritone? Was it the comfort in his gaze? Was it the tug of his lips into a reassuring smile?

As they managed to settle Rowena onto a stretcher and get her and her boys installed in the ambulance Stacey felt the beginnings of fatigue starting to set in.

'You're not coming with us?' Rowena asked, looking at Stacey from the stretcher.

'We'll meet you at the hospital,' Stacey consoled her. 'You're in good hands.' With a warm smile, she waited while Pierce closed the rear doors of the ambulance, then stepped away from the road, able finally to turn her attention to her own situation.

Why had Jasmine been so scared? Was Nell really OK? Were George and Lydia traumatised? Had Samantha coped all right?

She turned around, expecting to find Pierce next to her, but instead he was already heading over to where Nell was sitting on the picnic rug, still looking completely dazed. He carried her emergency kit on his back and the instant he reached Nell's side he knelt down and opened the bag.

'Let's take a closer look at your ankle,' he told her, brushing some hair from his sister's eyes.

'What happened? Why was there a fire?'

'She's been asking the same questions over and over,' Samantha volunteered as Stacey knelt down next to Pierce.

'She does that when she's upset. Even if you give her the answer it's too much for her to process.' Pierce gave his sister a hug. 'It's OK, Nell. Pierce is here. Pierce will look after you.'

'Always?' Nell's voice was soft, small and very little. It was as though the child within her was all that was available, and it showed just how vulnerable Nell really was when her world was unbalanced from its axis.

Stacey watched as Pierce smiled brightly at his sister. 'Always.'

She understood the bond between brother and sister and she was incredibly proud to see it. He was an honourable man who understood the importance of family. As she watched him tenderly review Nell's ankle, re-bandaging it and then scooping her up and carrying her to his car, Stacey felt her heart fill with a quiet, unassuming love. She wanted this man in her life. No. She *needed* Pierce in her life. She loved him with all her heart and she never wanted him to leave her.

CHAPTER NINE

AT THE HOSPITAL they met up with the burns registrar, who was able to give them an update on Trev.

'They're taking him to Theatre now, to debride and clean his wounds as best as possible, but the full extent of his injuries won't really be known for a few more days.'

Pierce nodded. 'Thanks for the information. We'll let his wife know.'

'Is Nell back from Radiology?' Stacey asked as they walked out of the Emergency Surgical Suite back towards the Emergency Department.

'No. The orthopaedic registrar told me they'd page me when she was done.'

His walk was brisk, but his shoulders seemed to be drawn further back than before and there was a constant furrow to his brow. They headed to the cranio-facial unit, where Rowena had been taken after admission. Thankfully her neighbour had come and collected her boys, so at least she didn't have to worry too much about them and could concentrate on what was happening to her.

'What about *your* children?' Rowena asked Stacey and Pierce after they'd passed on the news about Trev's condition.

'Sorry?' Stacey frowned, looking at the other woman blankly.

'Well, it must be difficult for the two of you to look after your own children when both of you end up here at the hospital all the time.'

'Oh. Those children.' Stacey nodded, belatedly realising what Rowena was talking about.

Before she could say another word, Pierce indicated the physical space existing between himself and Stacey.

'We're not married and those aren't our children,' he stated matter-of-factly.

Stacey's brow was once more creased in a frown, but this time it was because she didn't understand his tone. Yes, what he'd said was accurate and true—but it had been the *way* he'd said it…as though there was no possibility of the two of them ever being anything more than they were right now… Which was what? Boyfriend and girlfriend? Forever dating but never moving forward?

She remembered the first day she'd met Pierce. When she'd asked him if he was married, his answer had been an emphatic no. Was that how he felt? Did he still think like that? That matrimony wasn't for him?

She pushed the thoughts aside, knowing she was probably overthinking things again. And besides, Pierce was no doubt still very worried about Nell. She quickly informed Rowena that the children they'd been with at the park were her siblings, and that their friend Samantha had taken them home. There was no need to add that Molly had been at home and had called Stacey to say that both George and Lydia were safe with her. Jasmine, however, had refused to leave Nell's side.

'Oh.' Rowena settled back onto the pillows and closed her eyes. 'That makes sense, I guess. Still, you two make a good couple.' And then she closed her eyes, the medication she'd been given causing her to doze off.

Pierce's pager sounded, and when he'd checked

the number he stated, 'It's Radiology. Nell's X-rays are ready.'

Stacey nodded and together they spoke with the cranio-facial registrar before heading back to Radiology. As they headed down one of the hospital's long corridors she looked at him with concern.

'Pierce?'

'Hmm?'

He didn't slow his pace, and when Stacey put her hand on his arm, indicating he should slow down for a moment, he glanced over at her with a hint of impatience.

'Pierce, what's wrong?' When he simply stared at her, looking at her as though she'd just grown an extra head, she tried again. 'Are you worried about Nell?'

'When am I *not* worried about Nell?' The words were wrenched from him, and he turned and started walking again. 'Even when Mum and Dad were alive I was always there for Nell. *Always.*'

'And that's what makes you such a good brother,' she added as she caught up with him.

Pierce exhaled slowly, adjusting his pace a little so he wasn't hurtling along the corridor like an out-of-control freight train. 'At the end of the day it's all about family.'

'And Nell's OK. Yes, she's hurt her ankle, and that's going to upset her routine, but she'll adjust. You'll help her. We all will.'

'I know.' Pierce raked a hand through his hair, then stopped, looking down at Stacey. 'You're right, of course. The main point is that she's fine. No point in thinking what might have been, or how much worse the situation could have—' He stopped and shook his head. 'If a broken or—fingers crossed—badly sprained ankle is the worst thing that happens to her today, I'll take that.'

Stacey put her hands on his shoulders, wanting to reassure him, to help him. 'And you're not alone. You have me and Molly, and Jasmine and George and Lydia to help, and no doubt Samantha's going to be there to support Nell, too.'

Pierce nodded and drew her into his arms, but before he did Stacey looked into his eyes and saw such doubt as she'd never seen in him before. Doubt? Was he still doubting that Nell's ankle was only sprained? Did he think it was indeed broken? Or was there something else going on in his head that she simply wasn't privy to?

His arms around her, however, felt as warm and as strong and as comforting as always, and she quickly dismissed her thoughts. He was her strong, dependable Pierce once more. But he was also a man who was very concerned for his sister, and that made her love him all the more.

'Thank you, Stace.'

He pulled back and brushed a kiss across her lips, right there in the middle of the hospital corridor. She still wasn't used to such public displays of affection, but she was learning not to care what everyone else might think. She knew in her heart that the way she felt about Pierce was like nothing she'd ever felt before. And if she wanted to experience the full scope of what those emotions might be she couldn't be concerned with what other people might think of her relationship with him. It was no one else's business but their own.

'That's what friends are for,' she murmured as he kissed her again. When he smiled at her, the doubt she thought she'd seen had vanished and he was back to being his usual jovial and optimistic self.

'You,' he murmured, kissing her mouth once more before pulling back and taking her hand in his, 'are a very good friend, Dr Wilton.'

'I try my best, Dr Brolin,' she returned, and they headed to Radiology for the verdict on Nell's ankle.

When they arrived it was to find Jasmine sitting on Nell's hospital bed, teaching Nell a hand-clap game.

Nell seemed enthralled, determined to figure out the movements and then laughing along with Jasmine when she made a mistake.

'It's so good to see her laughing again,' Pierce murmured as he let go of Stacey's hand.

'I made a mistake.' Nell grinned widely when she saw Pierce and Stacey walking towards her.

Stacey smiled back at Nell, her heart warming to see Jasmine interacting with others again, but as soon as Jasmine realised Stacey was in the room she clammed up tight, the laughter disappearing, the smile slipping from her face.

Stacey frowned, completely perplexed by her sister's behaviour. Thankfully Pierce didn't seem to notice as he walked over and kissed the top of Nell's head.

'How are things going here?' he asked.

'I made a mistake,' Nell said again, laughing a little, before encouraging Jasmine to do the hand-clap routine again. Jasmine acquiesced and Stacey and Pierce watched as the two girls did the routine. When Nell managed it faultlessly, she cheered and wriggled in bed with delight. 'I solved the puzzle!' It was only after she moved that she winced in pain, having temporarily forgotten that she'd hurt her ankle.

'Steady, Nellie.' Pierce put a hand on her shoulders. 'Nice and still, remember?'

'Oh. Yes.' She nodded earnestly, but still wanted to do the hand-clap routine again and again.

'Let's see how *slowly* we can do it, Nell,' Jasmine suggested, and Stacey could have kissed her sister.

She had no idea what was really going on inside Jasmine's head, but she was a good girl at heart. Of that there was no doubt.

'Pierce. There you are,' said the radiographer as she came back into the room. 'Did you want to have a look at the X-rays? I've got them up on the screen.'

'Thanks.' Pierce and Stacey headed over to the computer monitor and stared at the X-rays. 'She *has* broken it.' His tone was a little despondent.

'But it's a clean break,' Stacey pointed out.

'Six weeks in a plaster cast. Crutches. Protective medical boot after that.' Pierce raked a hand through his hair again and that look of doubt returned to his eyes. What could it mean?

'Her recovery should be uneventful, and at your house ramps have been installed for Loris's wheelchair, so that will make it easier for her to manoeuvre about with her crutches.'

'I'll have to call her work and let them know what's happened. Once she's OK to go back I'll organise taxis to take her to and from the office. Then—'

'Pierce.' Stacey interrupted, taking his hand in hers and giving it a gentle squeeze. 'Breathe. It's OK. You don't have to figure out all the logistics right this second. Just be with Nell, reassure her. She'll be fine because she has you.'

He looked down at her as though he'd completely forgotten she was there. 'She doesn't take to change easily,' he said softly, so Nell couldn't hear him. 'The slightest thing, if it isn't handled correctly, can set her off. And once she's unsettled it can take days, weeks, even months to bring her back around.'

'I understand.' She gave his hand what she hoped was another reassuring squeeze. 'But you're not alone any more. I'm here—along with my plethora of siblings.' Stacey pointed to Jasmine. 'Just look at the two of them connecting. Jasmine talks more to Nell than she does to *anyone* else at the moment. This is a good thing—for both of them. Jasmine will be able to help Nell adjust.'

'Yeah. Yeah, you're right.'

He returned the squeeze on her fingers before releasing her, but Stacey could tell he was still very upset. He thanked the radiologist and asked if he could take Nell round to the plaster room to get the cast sorted out.

'The sooner I can take her home, the better,' he rationalised.

'Absolutely.' The radiographer was fine with that, but as Stacey had been the one to admit

Nell officially, given that Pierce was her brother, it was up to her to sign the necessary forms.

'Can I stay with her?' Jasmine's sullen tones were directed at Stacey.

'Sure. You'll need to get off her bed when we wheel it, but that would be great, Jazzy. Thanks.'

'Yes. Thanks for keeping Nell company,' Pierce added, placing one hand on Stacey's shoulder and smiling gratefully at Jasmine.

As they watched, Jasmine's gaze seemed to hone in on Pierce's hand before she glared at them both and carefully slid from Nell's bed. She glanced towards the door, then back to Nell, as though she really wanted to bolt, to leave, to be anywhere except where she was right now. But she also knew that wasn't at all fair to Nell. Instead, she gave Stacey one more glare before pointedly refusing to look at her any more.

'I am completely perplexed by her behaviour,' Stacey told Pierce quietly as they stood off to one side in the plaster room, watching as Nell had her ankle plastered into position. The young woman was delighted to have chosen a pink cast, but the decision had only come after a lot of debate and discussion with Jasmine.

'I think I know what might be causing it,' he remarked.

'Really?' Stacey turned to look at him.

'It's me.' Pierce took his time, turning his head from what was happening to his sister to look at Stacey. 'She resents my presence.'

'No. She was like this before you and I…you know…'

That small, sexy smile twitched at the corner of his mouth and she was instantly swamped with a flood of tingles, which then set off a chain reaction of sparks igniting in every part of her being.

'Before you and I…what?' he asked, his tone deep and intimate.

'Pierce.' She playfully hit his arm, feeling highly self-conscious and trying to stop her cheeks from blushing.

His warm chuckle surrounded her and she couldn't help but sigh at the sound. How was it he could make her feel so completely feminine with just one look, one sound, one touch? 'It's nice to see your smile,' she whispered.

'You didn't answer my question,' he continued, his deep drawl thrilling her so much that another wave of tingles surrounded her.

Stacey met and held his gaze, wanting to capture moments like this when he seemed less burdened, more playful, less troubled, more sexy.

'Before you and I...?' he proffered as a lead-in.

'Became...*involved*,' she finished, and smiled at him.

'Involved, eh?'

Stacey giggled, but Pierce nodded towards Jasmine.

'See? As soon as you laughed she glared across at us. She doesn't like me.'

'She doesn't *know* you,' Stacey remarked.

Still, it probably wouldn't be a bad idea if she tried once more to talk to Jasmine, to try and get her to open up. Perhaps with everything that had happened today the pressure might have built up enough for the teenager to explode.

'Jazzy's a lot like me. Cora says that's why we clash. We both store our stress in a bottle— shoving everything down, adding pressure to stop things from affecting us. But in the end those bottles become too full and the pressure gets too great, so that one tiny little innocuous event ends up having an over-dramatic and out-of-proportion response.'

'So in order to deal with this it's best to let her "explode"?'

'It's best to let her proverbial *bottle* explode, to release the pressure—because once the pressure's released only then is there any room for the clean-out to begin.'

'Your psychology professors would have been thrilled with such an explanation.'

'Shh,' she chided. 'This is how I've explained it to Jasmine over the years, so she can hopefully begin to understand what's happening to her and start to deal with the small things by herself.'

'Will she see a psychologist?'

Stacey shook her head. 'I've tried.'

'Would you mind if I had a go?' he asked as the plaster technician began tidying up, now Nell's ankle was firmly secured in the pink plaster cast. 'Why don't I take Jasmine to the pharmacy to pick up a pair of crutches? You can organise the paperwork for Nell's discharge. We'll meet you back in the ED.'

'OK. It's just as well you're here, because otherwise Nell would have needed to stay in over-night for observation.'

The words were nothing more than a throw-away comment as Stacey reluctantly left his side and headed towards Nell and Jasmine. As he'd presumed, Jasmine was a little reluctant to spend any time alone with him, but when Nell seemed eager to have her collect her crutches Jasmine agreed.

'Thanks again for staying with Nell,' Pierce started as they walked along the hospital cor-ridor.

'Yeah.'

'She doesn't have many close friends.'

'But she goes to work. She has a job.'

'A job that has been carefully structured in order to keep Nell's world as smooth as possible. A lot of the people who work with her are nice and polite, but they're not really her friends—or not what you and I might call friends.'

'I don't have *any*.'

Instead of contradicting her, telling her she had a lot of people who cared about her, who loved her, he didn't say anything. Jasmine looked at him expectantly, a little puzzled as to why he hadn't stated the obvious.

They walked on in silence until they reached the pharmacy. Pierce handed over the request for the crutches and when they had them they set off back the way they'd come.

'Ever been on crutches?' Pierce asked, a slight lift to his eyebrow.

'No.'

He smiled. 'Want to have a turn?'

Jasmine looked at him with stunned amazement. 'But I can't. They're Nell's.'

'Not yet.'

'Stacey will get mad.'

'I don't think so.' Pierce shook his head. 'Don't be too hard on your sister. Her life isn't all that easy.'

'But she's got everything she wants. She wanted to move back to Newcastle, so we did. She wanted to open up our dad's old surgery, so she did. She wanted to find a husband, so she did.' Jasmine gestured angrily to him.

Pierce's eyes widened a bit at the last statement but he didn't say anything. Instead he stopped walking and Jasmine followed suit, crossing her arms in front of her and adopting a stance that indicated she just didn't care.

He adjusted the height of the crutches so they were right for Jasmine and held them out to her. 'Here you go. They don't sit directly under your armpits, just a little lower. There. That's it.' He gave her some basic instructions to follow and waited for her to accept the crutches.

Her wide eyes conveyed her scepticism but she did as he'd suggested, fitting the crutches into place and then starting off carefully, keeping both feet on the ground while she adjusted to the feel of these foreign objects.

'Sometimes,' he said as they started slowly along the corridor, 'we all need a little help. Even Stacey.'

'Stacey's perfect. Always has been.'

'Stacey's heart is breaking.'

'Why? What did you do?' Jasmine's snarl was instant and she nearly overbalanced on the crutches. She concentrated and righted herself.

'*I* didn't hurt her.'

'Not yet.' The angry words were out of Jasmine's mouth before she could stop them. 'You'll hurt her. Robert hurt her.' Jasmine swallowed, starting to choke up a little. 'I heard her crying once. She thought everyone was asleep but I wasn't. She was in pain.' Jasmine angrily brushed a tear from her eyes. 'I don't want to be in pain like that. *Ever.* I'm going to be stronger than Stacey. I'm going to make sure that no one can make me cry. I'm going to make sure that I can stand on my own two feet and not need anyone else to prop me up. Like Nell, I'll be independent.'

'That sounds very lonely.'

'Nell's not lonely.'

'Because she allows other people to help her.' He indicated the crutches. 'It's all about balance.'

As he said the words to Jasmine he wondered if his own life was out of balance. Certainly today's events had jolted things a little.

Pierce waited for a moment, then started walking slowly again. Jasmine followed, still using the crutches. 'Have you ever asked Stacey why she was crying?'

'No.'

'Why not?'

'Because…because…' Jasmine started to pick up her pace on the crutches, hopping along quite confidently now. 'She wouldn't tell me anyway. I'm just a *kid*. They all stop talking when I come into the room. They hate me.'

'Maybe they're protecting you. Show them you're ready to listen.'

'How do I do that?'

Pierce grinned widely. 'You're a smart girl, Jasmine. You'll figure it out.' Then he looked up and down the corridor. 'Hey,' he said conspiratorially. 'There aren't many people in the corridor. Want to see how fast you can go on those crutches?'

Jasmine stared at him with shocked delight. 'Can I do that?'

Pierce waved her words away. 'Why not? Look around you. Assess the risks.' He ticked the points off on his fingers. 'And stop before you fall over.'

Jasmine smiled brightly, reminding him a lot of her gorgeous big sister. 'Isn't it silly?'

'Sometimes a bit of silly is good for the soul. Ready?'

The teenager nodded and checked the long corridor to make sure she wouldn't be getting in anyone's way.

'OK. Go!'

Pierce walked beside Jasmine, keeping well clear of the crutches. By the time they neared the ED Jasmine was laughing. He looked up and saw Stacey standing in the corridor, watching her sister use the crutches, watching her sister laughing. Stacey grasped her hands to her chest in delight. However, the instant Jasmine saw her sister she lost her rhythm and would have come a cropper if Pierce hadn't been there to steady her.

'Well done!' He picked up the crutch she'd dropped and accepted the other one from her as Jasmine quickly tried to school herself back into sullen teenager pose number one.

Stacey came over and placed her hands on Jasmine's shoulders. 'Are you OK?'

'Fine.'

Jasmine tried to shrug Stacey's hands away, but this time Stacey wasn't letting her. Instead she pulled Jasmine close, wrapping her arms around her sister.

'It's so good to see you laughing again. I've missed that sound so much.'

'You're not mad?'

'Mad?' Stacey pulled back. 'Why would I be mad?'

'Because I was being silly with the crutches.'

Stacey looked at Pierce and then back to her sister. 'Well, sometimes a little bit of silliness is good for the soul.'

'Here.' Pierce held the crutches out to Jasmine. 'Why don't you take these to Nell? You can demonstrate how to use them, but don't let her have a go on them just yet.'

'OK.' Jasmine accepted the crutches, a little perplexed as to why she was being given such responsibility, but doing it nevertheless.

'The nurse is with Nell,' Stacey remarked, jerking her thumb over her shoulder. 'I've signed the papers, so as soon as Nell is ready she can go home.'

'Thank you.'

'No.' Stacey slid her arms around his waist and hugged him close, not caring who saw them or what anyone said. Pierce had helped Jasmine to laugh again, and that not only filled Stacey with hope for her sister but also filled her heart with love for this wonderful, caring and clever man. 'Thank *you*.'

Pierce wrapped his arms around her, delighted she didn't seem to care who saw them. Given the eventful day they'd had thus far, everyone he cared about was safe. Yet there was one niggling thought that continued to churn around in his mind.

'I didn't hurt her.'

'Not yet.'

Jasmine fully expected him to hurt Stacey, to break Stacey's heart…and he had the sinking feeling she might be right.

CHAPTER TEN

THANKFULLY NELL RESPONDED well to the analgesics Stacey had prescribed, so now she was asleep, her plastered leg propped up on a few pillows, Pierce was able to relax a little. Jasmine was insisting on sleeping over in the spare bed in Nell's room.

'I'm not leaving her,' Jasmine said in a stage whisper when Stacey tried to beckon her from the room. 'I want to make sure she's OK through the night.'

Jasmine raised her chin defiantly and crossed her arms over her chest, almost daring Stacey to forcibly remove her. Instead Stacey's eyes filled with tears of pride, and for the second time in as many hours she hauled her sister close in an embracing hug.

'You're such a little warrior. I love that about you.' Stacey sniffed and then released Jasmine. 'Of course you must stay. I'm so proud that you want to—so proud of the way you protect Nell. Thank you, Jaz.' Stacey cleared her throat before making sure the spare bed in Nell's room was made up. 'Just sleep in your clothes and I'll bring you over some clean ones in the morning. Call me if you need anything.' She waited while Jasmine climbed into the bed. 'Is your phone charged?'

'Yeah.' Jasmine's puzzled eyes continued to stare at Stacey. 'Why are you being so nice to me?'

Stacey laughed a little at that and bent to kiss Jasmine's forehead. 'Because I love you, silly.'

With that, Stacey left the two girls to sleep, having already said goodnight to Samantha, who'd been very eager to get to her own bed after such a hectic day.

'Cup of tea?' Pierce asked as she walked into the kitchen.

'Yes, please.'

In silence he made the tea, both of them lost in their thoughts. 'Shall we sit on the veranda?' he asked, and when she nodded he carried their cups outside. Stacey sat down on the porch swing before accepting the cup from him.

They sat there for a while, with the clear night sky spread before them. When she'd finished her tea Pierce took her cup from her and slipped his arm around her shoulders. Stacey leaned closer, more than content to snuggle close to the man who had stolen her heart. Closing her eyes, she breathed him in, wanting to memorise every detail, every sensation he evoked within her. How was it possible she'd ever thought herself in love before?

With Pierce, she felt…*complete*. And because of that she felt confident. She didn't care who saw them together, who commented on their relationship or where things might end up. Pierce had helped her to realise she was a good person, and that at times she was too hard on herself, mentally berating herself when things didn't work out the way she'd envisioned. He made her feel like a person of worth, someone *he* wanted to spend his time with, to share his life with.

As she sat there, relaxing in his arms, allowing herself to dream of a perfect future side by side with Pierce, she felt him tense. 'What is it?' she murmured softly.

'Huh?'

'You just tensed.'

'Oh. Did I?' He shifted on the porch swing, almost overbalancing them. Forcing a laugh, he stood up and walked out to the garden. The grass was soft beneath his feet. Soon summer would come, the grass would dry and turn brown, but for now, thanks to the lovely spring weather they'd enjoyed, everything was good. 'I was just thinking about Nell…about how things could have been worse.'

'But they weren't.'

'I know, I know. But worrying about her is a hard habit to break.' He exhaled harshly. 'There are just so many things that will need to change now, and any change can trigger a decline into tantrums. She becomes so single-minded, she can't understand why I can't change things back.'

He spread his arms wide.

'When our parents died she kept demanding I go and pick them up. For months, Stacey. *Months.* Every single day. And every single day when I had to tell her that I couldn't do it, that I couldn't just get in my car and go and pick them up like she wanted me to, my heart would break. Months this went on.'

'Oh, Pierce.' Stacey stood and walked over to him, wrapping her arms about his waist and hugging him close. 'What you must have gone through—and here I am complaining about Jasmine's attitude when really I have nothing to complain about at all.'

'Your challenges are different, but you still have every right to complain, Stace.' His tone was gentle as he dropped a kiss to her head, but then he unhooked her arms from about his waist and walked further into the shadows of the night. 'My mind is trying to process everything, trying to consider every angle, every contingency that needs to be put in place in order to make Nell's recovery as smooth as possible.'

'I know everything's a bit of a jumble now, but it'll work itself out.'

'What if she endures a setback? What if this event means she's unable to live independently?'

'Well, Samantha's here now, and Loris is due to move in within the next few weeks, isn't she?'

'Yes, but that is also change. And too much change...' He stopped and sighed again.

Stacey watched him for a moment, her mind trying to process what he was saying. She understood that too much variety wasn't good for Nell, but things wouldn't always go to plan in the future—wasn't it best simply to deal with things as and when they arose? In fact, now that she thought about it, with Nell's second house-mate due to move in soon it would mean that the three-bedroom home was quite full.

'Where are you planning to live?' The question left her lips before she could stop it and she quickly tried to explain. 'Sorry. I'm blurting things out again. But it just occurred to me that once Nell's other housemate moves in there'll be no room for you.'

'Correct. Initially I planned to rent somewhere nearby—just a one-bedroom flat—until after Christmas, and then I was due to head overseas.'

'But you're not going now?' Even as she said the words the thought of Pierce living on the other side of the world choked at her heart.

'I haven't planned on it. And I'm glad I *did* turn down the job when they re-offered it to me.'

'When, exactly, did they approach you?'

'They emailed me a few weeks ago and asked me to start next month.'

'What did you say?'

'I said no, of course.'

She frowned as she thought things through. 'How long have they been offering you this position?'

Pierce shook his head and walked towards the flowerbeds. 'Does it matter?' He bent down and breathed in the scent of the flowers.

'Yes, it does.'

At the insistence in her voice, he turned to face her.

'Why?'

'Because it's clear to see that you leaving and working alongside such an accomplished research team, working through a lot of the questions still surrounding adult autism, is something close to your heart. If they've been holding this job for you, offering it to you on a regular basis for years, then it's important that you go.'

As she spoke the words out loud Stacey felt as though she'd just plunged a knife through her own heart.

When Pierce didn't say anything, she swallowed and forced herself to continue. 'You write articles for them. You research on your own with limited resources. Just think of all the good you could do working alongside those other brilliant minds, utilising their funding, pooling your knowledge, making a real difference in the way society at large treats adults who are trying to integrate permanently into a normal functioning world.'

Pierce's answer was simply to shake his head.

'Hang on. You said you turned the job down a few weeks ago?'

'That's right and after tonight's events, I'm glad I did.'

'Why did you turn it down? Isn't this your dream job?' Pierce looked up at the star-lit sky for a moment, but before he could speak Stacey continued. 'Did you turn it down because of my medical practice?'

'I promised to help you until the end of the year, when Cora returns.'

'And I thank you for that. But it sounds to me as though the university wants you desperately, Pierce. And if that's the case, then go.' She tried to stop her voice from breaking on the last word and quickly cleared her throat in case he'd heard. 'I can get a locum in.'

'I *am* your locum, and I take my responsibilities seriously.'

'So do I—and I will not be the one to stand in the way of you accepting your dream job.'

Pierce stared at her as though she'd grown another head. 'Are you trying to get rid of me?'

Stacey closed her eyes, glad that it was dark and he couldn't see the tears she was desperately trying to hold back. 'If I have to.' She breathed in slowly, then let it out, unable to believe what she was about to say. 'If I have to fire you in order to get you to take that job then I will.' There was determination in her tone.

'But what about Nell?'

Stacey clenched her jaw, knowing that what she was about to do was for his own good. 'You've put everything in place as far as Nell is concerned, and while her fractured ankle might be a bit of a setback, and bring its own new level of logistics, you've still taught her how to cope with big changes. Plus it's not as though you'd be leaving tomorrow. I'll help you organise things, and we will be there for Nell, helping her every step of the way. Shortfield Family Medical Practice isn't only her closest GP surgery but my family and I are also her friends. We love Nell.'

'I know.' Pierce walked towards her and placed his hands on her shoulders. 'And I thank you, Stacey. I thank you from the bottom of my heart for the way you genuinely love my little sister.' He looked down into her face, half in shadow, half lit by the glow of the moon. 'You look so beautiful. You *are* so beautiful—not only physically but also within your heart.' He shook his head. 'You've changed my life and…and…it would be wrong of me to leave.'

'You have to.' She bit her lip to stop herself from crying. It was breaking her heart to say these words to him, especially when the last thing she really wanted was for him to leave her.

'No. Catherine left me to further her career, and I thought it was incredibly selfish of her. It's just a job, Stacey. I'm not going to sacrifice what's important to me simply because of a job.'

'You couldn't be selfish if you tried, Pierce. And where Catherine's concerned you've told me yourself she's done amazing work, helped so many people. But when you think back to your relationship, perhaps she simply used her career as an excuse because she knew deep down inside that things weren't right.' She swallowed. 'I lied to myself where Robert was concerned, telling myself he'd change after we were married, that I could live with my career always playing second fiddle to his, that I could be restrained as far as being demonstrative in my love for him went. I was willing to settle and it was wrong of me. Robert hurt me when he left me at the altar, and I wish he'd been more upfront with me, telling me his decision *before* I left for the church, but in hindsight his selfish actions saved us both from a lifetime of misery.'

She closed her eyes again, a single tear falling from her lashes to roll down her cheek.

'I couldn't bear it if you always regretted putting me before this job.'

She trembled when Pierce brushed the tear from her cheek.

'I won't.'

'You can't say that. It's been your dream, and you've already devoted so much of your time to it. I've read the articles you've written and you can do so much more with the research team behind you.' She looked up at him, not caring that a few more tears slid down her cheeks. 'Go. Do the work you're meant to do.'

'But, Stacey—'

'No. You're fired, Pierce.'

'You're not serious.' He laughed without humour as she stepped away from his touch.

'I am.'

'No. You're just doing this because you think it's the right thing to do. Well, you can't push me into this decision, Stacey. I'll be turning up to work next week, same as always.'

'No, you won't.'

'But you won't be able to cope.'

'Of course I'll cope. I'm the queen of coping.' She sniffed and brushed away a few of the tears from her cheeks. 'I know what it's like to work in your dream job. I'm doing it right now. Running my dad's old medical practice has been my dream since I was fourteen years old, and although my selfishness might have caused some of my family members—namely Jasmine— a lot of pain, the thrill of finally being where I'm meant to be, of achieving those life-long goals—'

She broke off and smiled.

'It's…amazing. For the first time in my life I know I'm exactly where I need to be and it feels great.' She shook her head. 'I won't be the one to deny *you* experiencing that same sensation, and I'm sure if Nell had a full grasp of the situation then she wouldn't want that either. Both of you have worked so hard to get her to this stage of independent living. Years and years of work, and Nell is ready for you to go. It's what she's expecting and you risk confusing her further if you *don't* go.'

Before he could say another word she turned and headed into the house, wiping at her eyes in order to clear her vision. She located her bag and car keys before turning and heading back out again.

'You're leaving?' Pierce was half on the veranda, half on the threshold as she walked past him.

'I need to.' Before she made a complete fool of herself and begged him not to listen to a word she was saying.

'Stacey—wait.'

She unlocked her car and put her bag inside

before turning to face him, the driver's door between them.

'What about us? Isn't what we feel for each
other worth pursuing?'

She reached out and placed a hand to his cheek,
determined she wouldn't cry. 'If you love someone, set them free.' She smiled lovingly at the
man who had stolen her heart, now and for ever
more. 'You are going to be amazing. You are
going to achieve such great things—and those
great things are going to help so many people. I
could never stand in the way of that.'

Her voice broke, and before she completely lost
her resolve to set him free she turned from him,
climbed into the car, shut the door and started
the engine.

'Stacey!'

She tried not to hear the pleading in his tone
as she carefully reversed out of the driveway,
only belatedly remembering to switch on her
headlights. Even though they lived only a few
blocks from each other she still had to pull over
to wipe her tear-filled eyes because she couldn't
see properly.

When she reached her house she headed quietly for her bedroom and, uncaring that she hadn't changed or brushed her teeth, she lay down on her bed and allowed the tears to fall. She loved him. She loved Pierce with all her heart. But she could never live with herself if he sacrificed his own dreams for her. His dreams were his, and he deserved the chance to achieve them.

'If you love someone, set them free. If they come back to you, they're yours. If they don't, they never were.' She recited the quote into her pillow, hoping amongst hope that one day Pierce would return to her—because she would always be waiting for him.

'Good morning, sleepy-head,' Molly remarked as she came into Stacey's bedroom. 'Or should I say good afternoon?' Molly put a cup of tea on the bedside table, then walked to the window, where she opened the blind to let a bit of mid-day light flood into the room.

'What?' A groggy Stacey lifted her head from the pillow, trying to open her bleary eyes. 'What time is it?' She put out a hand to search for her bedside clock, but nearly upset the cup of tea in the process.

'Steady on. It's half-past twelve.'

'Oh, my goodness—Jasmine!' Stacey sat bolt upright in bed. 'I was supposed to take her clean clothes and pick her up hours ago.'

'Chillax, sis. It's fine. Jaz called and asked if she could stay until later this afternoon. She said she was having fun helping Nell adjust and teaching her, with Samantha's help, how to use the crutches properly. Still, I thought you were probably going to go and check on Nell anyway, and besides, it gives you more time to play cutesey kissey-face with Pierce.' Molly grasped her hands theatrically to her chest and then sighed dramatically. 'Oh, most beloved, take me in your arms and kiss me until I see stars.'

'Knock it off, Molly.' Stacey slumped back down onto the pillows.

'Wait. I know *that* tone. What's wrong?' Molly came over and sat on Stacey's bed. 'What's happened?'

'It's over.'

'Between you and Pierce? But how? But why? But yesterday everything was peachy.'

'I'm not sure I want to talk about it right now, Molly.' Stacey rested her hand across her eyes. 'Would you mind doing Nell's check-up when you pick up Jasmine?'

'Isn't that the coward's way out? Besides, Nell will be expecting you.'

'Ugh!' Stacey picked up a spare pillow and put it over her face, yelling her frustration into it.

She knew Molly had a point—that Nell would be confused if Stacey didn't turn up to do the check-up and right now the last thing Nell needed was to have even more instability—but the thought that Stacey would probably bump into Pierce when she went was something she simply didn't want to face right now.

Molly lifted the pillow off her. 'I *hate* always doing what's right. I hate it, Molly.'

'Are you afraid you'll see Pierce when you go?'

'Of course I am.' Stacey flicked back the bedcovers and stepped out of bed, heading to the bathroom. When she came back it was to find Molly sipping at the teacup. 'I thought that was for me.'

'You're clearly in no mood to drink a relaxing cup of peppermint tea. You need coffee, my soul sister, so why don't you have a shower and I'll make you one? Then George, Lydia and I, along with the rabbits as a diversion for Nell, will come with you to the Brolins' house and run interference for you so that you don't have to speak to Pierce.'

Stacey relaxed a little and rushed over to hug her sister, almost making Molly spill the tea. 'Thank you. I knew I could count on you.'

'Always.'

Stacey got dressed and had something to eat, while Molly organised the children and the animals, then drove them all round to Nell's house.

'I just love walking up this path,' Molly said. 'It really does bring back so many wonderful memories. I'm glad someone we love is living in this house and making it her home. It's like the house is ready to make the next generation of memories.'

Stacey didn't reply. She was too focused on looking around the garden, half expecting Pierce to pop out from behind a bush, wearing the same gardening clothes he'd been wearing that first day she'd met him. It seemed so long ago, yet in reality she'd known Pierce for less than two months. Still, in her heart it felt as though she'd known him for a lot longer.

When she entered the house she looked around quickly, but still there was no sign of him. Jasmine and Nell were seated at the table, doing some puzzles. Samantha was in the kitchen baking.

'I like baking when I'm feeling stressed or a little out of sorts,' the woman told them as she checked the cupcakes she had in the oven. 'Besides, I know these ones are Nell's favourite, because when I bring them to work she tells me they're her favourite, so I thought, why not make some to help cheer her up?'

'Good idea,' Stacey remarked, smiling as Nell's eyes lit up upon seeing the rabbits, as well as George and Lydia but more so the rabbits. Stacey wasn't going to ask where Pierce was, or even if he was there. She was just going to do her job and then, if Molly wanted to chat, Stacey would head next door to check on Mike and Edna. But thankfully it was Jasmine who gave her the information she sought.

'Pierce isn't home at the moment. He got called

into the hospital this morning and that's why I said I'd stay with Nell.'

'Oh.' Stacey was both relieved and disappointed at the same time. She didn't want to see Pierce and yet she yearned to see him. She loved him so much. 'Right, well…Nell, let's get your check-up over and done with. When you've finished that puzzle I need to check your blood pressure and your foot—'

'And listen to my heart?' Nell asked. 'Can I listen to my heart? Pierce sometimes lets me listen to my heart. It goes ba-dum, ba-dum.'

Stacey smiled. 'Of course you can listen to your heart.'

The check-up didn't take too long, and when Samantha asked if they'd like to stay for Sunday afternoon snack-time Molly raised a questioning eyebrow in Stacey's direction.

'Sure. Why not?' she remarked, hoping against hope that Pierce didn't return from the hospital while they were still there.

Thankfully she managed to enjoy a leisurely afternoon tea and say her goodbyes to Nell and Samantha.

Jasmine was quiet on the drive home, and it

wasn't until they walked in the door and waited while George and Lydia took the rabbits back to their hutch, that she turned to Stacey and demanded, 'What's going on with you and Pierce?'

Stacey blinked, a little taken aback. 'Pardon?'

'Pierce looked half sick this morning, all pale and grey, as though he'd eaten something terrible. I asked him if he was OK and he just said, "Yeah." But I could tell there was more wrong than he was saying. And then when you came you were like a mouse being chased by a cat, and *you* looked all pale and grey, too.'

Molly placed her hands on Jasmine's shoulders, then kissed her sister's cheek. 'She's not just a pretty face.'

Jasmine merely stared at Stacey, as if to say she wasn't moving until she got an explanation.

'Well…uh…Pierce and I are…well, we're going to stop seeing each other for a while.'

'You're not going to stop me from seeing Nell?' Again there was that defiant, adamant tone.

'No. Of course not. Nell needs you—well, needs all of us—now more than ever.'

'What? What do you mean?'

Stacey took a deep breath, then looked at Molly, and then back to Jasmine. 'Pierce is heading overseas.'

'What?' Molly and Jasmine spoke in unison.

'Nell will soon be living independently, just as she's always wanted.'

'And Pierce will be free to do whatever he wants?'

There was disgust in Jasmine's tone, and Stacey held up her finger in reprimand.

'Pierce is an amazing man who has done a lot of research and written many scientific papers on the subject of adult autism—especially with regard to integration.'

'I know what integration is,' Jasmine said, before either of her sisters could explain. 'Remember the school I went to in Perth? The school I loved? My friends I loved, whether they had a disability or not?'

'Yes. Of course. Well, Pierce has been offered a job in America and…he's going to take it. When he's there,' she went on before Jasmine could say another word, 'he'll continue his work with regard to integration with an experienced team of researchers. The work he can do there will help thousands and thousands of adults with autism to be better accepted by society.'

Jasmine pondered Stacey's words for a moment, then crossed her arms over her chest and glared at them both. 'I don't see why he has to go to America to do that,' she said, then turned and stomped off to her bedroom.

'I get the feeling Jasmine really does like him,' Molly remarked as they both braced themselves for the ritual slamming of their sister's bedroom door.

Stacey slumped down into a chair and rested her head in her hands.

'Does he have to go?' Molly's question was quiet.

'Yes.'

'Do you want him to go?'

'Yes.'

'What? Why? I thought you were in love with the man.'

Stacey lifted her head and looked at her sister. 'It's *because* I'm in love with him that I'm making him go. He deserves the chance to fulfil his own dreams just like me moving here, or you doing surgery, or Cora going to Tarparnii, or

Nell living independently. Pierce has dedicated all his time and effort to Nell. He's a good man, with a big heart.'

'Will the two of you still stay together? I mean nowadays long-distance relationships aren't that difficult to maintain thanks to internet chats and emails and stuff.'

'I don't know.'

With that, Stacey stood and headed towards her own bedroom, to lie on her bed and cry some more.

CHAPTER ELEVEN

BY THE END of November Stacey was worn out. She went to work early in the morning and returned late most nights. She'd started a night clinic in an effort to catch up on the overflow of patients but also to give her time to ferry her siblings around to their various after-school activities. Most nights she collapsed into bed with exhaustion.

Molly helped at the clinic as much as she was able, but after an hour or two was often called in to the hospital, leaving Stacey and Winifred to cope with whatever patients were left.

'You can't go on like this,' Winifred said late one evening, giving Stacey a big hug. 'You'll work yourself into an early grave.'

'I know. But the new locum will start soon and then, come Christmas-time, Cora will be home.'

'It's a shame Pierce took that job in America before his contract here was up.'

'I fired him,' Stacey told her.

'What? Why would you do that?'

'Because he never would have left to follow his dreams otherwise.'

Winifred sighed and patted Stacey's arm. 'You really love him, don't you?' she stated.

'Yes.'

It was as simple and as complex as that. Yes, she loved him. Yes, she missed him. Yes, she wanted him back, to have her arms around him, to have his mouth pressed to hers.

'He'll be back before you know it,' Winifred promised. 'Go on home, love. I'll lock up.'

Stacey hoped Winifred was right—that Pierce would be back sooner rather than later. Before he'd left for the States he'd tried to contact her, but she hadn't wanted to take his calls. He'd emailed her but she hadn't wanted to read them. Cutting herself off from him was the only way she knew how to make the pain in her heart decrease.

Two weeks after Nell had broken her ankle, two weeks after Stacey had fired him and told him to head overseas, Pierce had been due to leave. The night before his flight she'd gone to bed early, not wanting to dwell on the way her heart ached for him. She'd awoken to the soft sound of someone knocking on her bedroom window and cautiously she'd peeked through the curtains, her heart swelling with love when she'd seen Pierce standing there.

Pulling on a dressing gown and slippers, she'd headed outside to see what he wanted, instantly concerned that something had happened to Nell.

'Is Nell all right?'

'Nell's fine. I'm not.' He'd hauled her into his arms and pressed his lips to hers in one swift movement that robbed her of breath. 'I've missed you these past weeks, Stacey. Why didn't you return my calls? My emails?'

'Pierce.' She tried to pull away from his arms but her efforts were half-hearted at best, because with all honesty that was the place she wanted to be the most. 'I can't do this.'

'What? Let me hold you? Let me kiss you? Stacey, I'm not going to see you for…I don't even want to think about it. I need this—these memories—to get me through.'

'I know, but I—'

He silenced her with another heart-melting

kiss, and this time Stacey couldn't help but cling to him. 'Oh, Pierce.'

'I don't know how to do this,' he told her.

'Do what?'

'Be selfish.'

'I know. You're the most giving man I've ever met.'

'And yet here I am, doing what *I* want to do.'

'For a change,' she finished. 'And, for the record, you're not being selfish. You're following your dreams and you deserve the chance to do it.'

'But what if this *isn't* my real dream? What if my dream has…changed?'

'You won't know for sure until you get to America.' She shook her head and kissed his lips. 'You'll have a great time,' she encouraged him, trying desperately to instil enthusiasm into her voice.

'It would be far greater if you were to come with me,' he said, but Stacey shook her head.

'It's not my dream, but I believe in you.'

He kissed her again. 'And that, my beautiful, wonderful, most beloved Stacey, is worth everything.'

'What time does your flight leave?' she asked.

'I need to leave for the airport in an hour.'

'Come and sit with me.' And so the two of them sat on the chairs on her small veranda, content to hold each other and look at the stars, thankful the October night was not too warm for cuddling.

When finally it came time for him to leave, Pierce kissed her with such passion that she swooned.

'Please take my calls while I'm overseas.'

'No.'

'What? Why not?'

'I can't bear to hear your voice or to see you over the internet because it'll just make me miss you more.' And she wasn't sure whether she'd be able to cope with that.

'OK, then. What about emails and text messages?'

Stacey thought about this for a moment, then nodded. 'Yes.'

'Good.' He exhaled happily before kissing her once more, then walking over to the hire car parked in her driveway.

She was glad he hadn't asked her to take him

to the airport, because there was no way she'd ever be able to say goodbye to him and then watch him get onto a plane and leave her. Even this, standing in her own driveway and crying as he drove away, was bad enough.

Now, six weeks since he'd left, Stacey still found it difficult to get out of bed every morning, knowing she wouldn't be seeing him at the clinic. Her dreams were always of him, and she lived for his emails, loving the excitement she read in his words about the research he was doing and the staff he was working with.

Nell's ankle had healed nicely, and all in all she'd coped with the disruption to her usual routine quite well—so much so that she'd refused to go back to catching the bus to and from work and now had a standing arrangement with the taxi company to pick her up every morning and drop her home every afternoon.

Jasmine still went round every afternoon after school, sometimes with George and Lydia and sometimes just by herself. Then, on Friday afternoons, Nell would join the rest of the Wilton family as they all headed over to Mike and Edna's for dinner, bringing the rabbits with them.

Mike would offer instruction and coaching in the art of encouraging rabbits to jump higher over an obstacle.

All in all, Stacey's days were jam-packed with family and patients and longing for Pierce, but when December arrived the days seemed even longer. More patients. More ferrying her siblings to and from their various after-school events. More stress, and most of all more missing Pierce.

'Cup of tea?'

Stacey opened her eyes where she sat, slumped on the sofa after another hard day at the clinic. She was surprised to see Jasmine standing before her, holding a piping hot cup of tea out to her.

'Oh, Jazzy.' Stacey was overwhelmed at the thoughtful gesture, but sat up straight and sighed with relief as she accepted the cup. 'You are a life-saver, my gorgeous sister. Thank you.'

Jasmine looked as though she, too, was about to burst into tears, and after Stacey had taken the cup the teenager hesitated for a moment, before sitting down next to Stacey.

'Mmm. That is a perfect cuppa.'

Jasmine grinned with happiness at the praise.

'It's good to see you smiling. That also helps in so many ways.' Stacey brushed her sister's hair back from her face. 'I've been so worried about you.'

'I was…' Jasmine bit her lip, hesitating.

Stacey waited intently.

'That day in the park, when Nell got hurt…'

'Yes?' It was a day Stacey could never forget. So much had transpired that day. So many emotions. 'What about it?'

'I thought I'd caused Nell to get hurt.'

'What?'

'I threw the Frisbee too far and she tried to get it, and it landed near that barbecue where the man was cooking, and if I hadn't thrown it there Nell wouldn't have been near it, and Nell getting hurt is all my fault.' Jasmine broke down into tears, covering her face with her hands.

Stacey instantly put her cup on the table and gathered her sister close. 'No. No, sweetie. It wasn't your fault. Not at all. There was absolutely no way you could have known what was going to happen. It was an accident. Not your fault at all. Oh, poor Jaz. Have you been carrying this burden with you all this time? Oh, honey.' Stacey started crying as well, feeling her sister's pain keenly.

'I was so angry at you for taking me away from my friends, for bringing us here. I wanted to punish you, and then when I saw Nell lying there...I...I...all I wanted was you. I wanted you to pick me up like you used to and cuddle me close and tell me everything would be all right.' Jasmine spoke through her tears, hiccuping now and then. 'I know Nell's OK now, but...but...'

Stacey fished around in her pockets for some tissues and managed to find two clean ones. 'I'm always here for you, Jaz. No matter what the circumstances. You're allowed to be angry with me, or Cora or Molly or any of us. You're entitled to your own emotions and to be able to show them. That's OK. We're sisters. We'll always work it out in the end because we love each other.'

'Pierce said you love me. He said that things are really difficult for you. And until he said that I hadn't really thought about it like that, you know? And now he's gone, and you're working lots, and you're really tired and you're unhappy, and I don't like seeing you like that. So I couldn't talk to you about Nell, but it was getting too much. That bottle you talk about—it was building up too much. And then…I just couldn't hold it in any more.'

A fresh bout of tears accompanied her words and Stacey held her sister, dabbing at her eyes.

'It's OK. I've got you. Everything's going to be all right,' she crooned, and after a while Jasmine stopped crying and blew her nose. Stacey followed suit and they both smiled. 'I do love you, Jaz. You're my sister. We're family. We're all we've got.'

'We've got Nell and Pierce now, too.' She covered her mouth with her hand. 'Oh, I forgot. Molly told me not to say his name around you in case it upset you too much, but—'

'It's fine. Molly's just being protective.'

'Do you need protecting?' Jasmine sat up straighter. 'Because I'll protect you, too.'

Stacey felt another wave of tears coming on—tears of happiness at seeing that fierce and determined spirit of her sister's shining forth yet again. 'Thank you. But I'm doing all right at the moment.'

'Do you miss him?'

'Of course. But it's important for people to follow their dreams.' She'd tried to keep her words strong but even she had heard the wobble in her voice. This time it was Jasmine who offered the hug, holding her big sister close, and Stacey loved every moment of it.

Jasmine sniffed. 'I love you, Stacey.'

'I love you, too. Always.' They both blew their noses again and then laughed. 'Look at us. Red eyes and red noses. We must look a sight.' Stacey stood and pulled Jasmine to her feet. 'How about some ice cream?'

'But…you haven't even had dinner.' Jasmine pointed to the kitchen. 'I've made a plate of food for you.'

'Thank you. You've been such a wonderful help. But at the moment I need ice cream. Comfort food.' Stacey headed to the kitchen. 'Want some?'

'Yeah.' Jasmine watched as her sister pulled out an ice cream tub and scooped some into bowls. 'I've never seen you like this before. All "break the rules", like.'

'Then it's about time you did.'

And that was how Molly found them an hour

later, when she arrived home from the hospital, exhausted. Stacey had finished her ice cream, then eaten her dinner, and Jasmine had kept her company.

'Kids asleep?' Molly asked as she kissed her sisters on the cheek.

'Yes,' Jasmine replied. 'George put himself to bed tonight—he was so tired after his karate lesson—and Lydia fell asleep with a book still in her hands.'

They all chuckled.

'Typical Lydia,' Molly remarked as she re-heated her dinner. 'Oh, I had a thought earlier today. How about next weekend we all do something together? A family activity. I'm not on call, and the kids will all be finished school for the year, so we should celebrate by doing something super-fun.'

'How about ice-skating?' Jasmine suggested.

'I'm not sure Nell knows how to ice-skate, and although her ankle has now healed I wouldn't want to risk her falling over and injuring it again.'

'Good point.' Jasmine nodded, pleased that

Nell was automatically included in their family plans.

'How about bowling?' Molly suggested a moment later.

'Bowling?' Jasmine's eyes lit up. 'I used to love it when Mum took us bowling. Yeah. Let's go bowling—Nell will love it.'

'Plus,' Molly added, hugging Stacey close, 'the local bowling alley has cheesy music videos.'

Stacey grinned and hugged her sister back. 'Sounds like the perfect tonic for me. The cheesier the better.'

The following weekend, with the children excited about being on school holidays for six weeks, Stacey completed her house calls in record time—especially as Jasmine had volunteered to come along and help out. They picked Nell up from her house—Samantha and Loris declined the invitation to join them—and then went home, where they met an excited George and Lydia bouncing around in the corridor.

'Where's Molly?' Stacey asked.

'She's in the bedroom on the telephone. She said she had some loose ends to tie up.'

'Oh?' Stacey hoped her sister hadn't been

called in to the hospital, but thankfully when Molly appeared a moment later she assured her sister that everything was fine and that they should head off before they missed their booking.

At the bowling alley they all enjoyed the game—Nell perhaps most of all. And seeing the delight on the young woman's face Stacey wished Pierce was there to see it. She took a photo on her phone of Nell's smiling face after she'd knocked all the pins down, then sent the picture to Pierce's phone.

'You all right?' Molly asked as she came and sat down next to Stacey while Lydia had a turn at bowling.

'Sure!' Stacey offered the word with fake brightness, pointing to the cheesy music video on the television monitors scattered around the bowling alley and the black lighting which made the fluorescent bowling balls stand out like neon. 'Glad I didn't wear white or I'd be glowing brightly under these lights, but the music videos are definitely worth it. Oh, the eighties! Those fashions! That hair!'

'It's fun.'

'It is. It was a good idea, Molly. Thank you.' Stacey hugged her sister.

'Uh…well, you may not want to thank me too much.'

Molly whispered the words in Stacey's ear and she felt a prickle of apprehension work its way down her spine. Stacey eased back and looked at her sister.

'Why?' she asked cautiously.

'Um…well…' The music video changed on the screen and Molly pointed to it. 'Look. Let's watch this one. Hey, kids. Let's watch this music video.'

'What's going on? Why are you acting so stran—?' Stacey wasn't able to finish her sentence as her eyes widened at what she was seeing on the television monitors.

It was Pierce. Larger than life. On every single television monitor in the bowling alley.

'What? But…how?'

Then she stared in utter shock as he started lip-syncing to one of her favourite songs—a song about love, trust and dedication to each other.

'Pierce made you a cheesy video,' Molly remarked quietly.

'He…*what*?'

'Just watch.'

And she did as Pierce, dressed in an all-white suit, holding a large bunch of red roses, was seen to be looking high and low for his one true love, searching for her everywhere, singing to the camera, his handsome face radiating an earnest and honest desire to find her. Stacey's jaw dropped open in stunned disbelief as she watched him knocking on the door to her house, but receiving no reply.

'When was this filmed? And…*how*?'

'We live in an age of digital technology, Stace,' Jasmine offered.

'Yeah. It's not hard,' George added, like the wise old man he was.

Nell was clapping along in time to the music, thoroughly delighted at seeing her big brother on the television. At the end of the video Pierce was still searching, and there was a shot of him walking to the front of the bowling alley. Stacey sat up straighter in her chair—then the television monitors went blank. But the music continued playing over the loudspeakers.

Now everyone in the bowling alley had stopped

bowling and they were all pointing and gasping in delight as the man from the video walked into the bowling alley, dressed in the pure white suit which became bright white beneath the black lights. He still carried the enormous bunch of red roses—Stacey's favourite—and headed slowly in her direction.

She stood, belatedly realising she was trembling. When he reached her side he smiled at her and held out the roses. A few people around them started clapping, but Stacey didn't hear them. All she was aware of was Pierce, standing before her, smiling brightly and placing the roses into her arms. What did it all mean?

She didn't have to wait long to find out.

When the music ended Pierce held out his hand for hers. Stacey shifted the roses onto one arm and gave him her hand, loving the feel of her hand securely in his. She bit her lip, her heart pounding with love for the man before her.

'Stacey. I've missed you so very much. Too much to be apart from you any longer. You encouraged me to follow my dreams and you were right when you said I'd feel a strong sense of accomplishment when I was finally in the right job in the right place at the right time…and that dream job is working alongside you in a small family-run GP clinic in Shortfield.'

'What?' She gaped at him. 'But what about Yale and your research and—?'

'All still good. All still happening. But happening on both sides of the world. I'm setting up a sister study at Newcastle General Hospital. I'll work part-time there and part-time with you at the clinic…but I'll be working *full time* in the best relationship, the happiest relationship I've ever had the pleasure to be in.' He shook his head slowly from side to side and gazed down into her eyes. 'I've missed you, Stacey. So much it started to physically hurt to be so far away from you.'

'Oh!' Stacey tried to blink back tears of happiness, not wanting to miss a second of seeing his handsome face, of hearing his perfect words.

Then, to her further astonishment, he released her hand for a moment to unbutton his white suit jacket, revealing a white T-shirt beneath. On the T-shirt was painted, in fluorescent pink writing, the words *Will you marry me?*

He went down on bended knee and took her

hand in his again. 'I love you, Stacey, and I intend to spend the rest of my life showing you that. I adore you. Please, will you do me the honour of becoming my wife?'

Stacey opened her mouth to speak but found her words choked with pure emotion, so she quickly nodded and tugged him to his feet, desperate to have his lips pressed against hers. 'Yes,' she finally whispered, just before he kissed her.

'I've missed you,' he returned. 'I love you. So very much.'

'You are my everything,' she told him, smiling with happiness when he tenderly brushed away a few escaped tears with his thumb.

Then somehow the flowers were removed from her arms and Pierce was hugging her close, kissing her passionately in front of anyone and everyone who happened to be in the bowling alley. The round of applause and whoops of joy from their siblings went unnoticed as both Stacey and Pierce only had eyes for each other.

'How did you like the music video?' he eventually asked when Nell had insisted on finishing her bowling game.

Stacey sat on her fiancé's lap, her arms around his neck as though never letting him go again.

'Cheesy enough for you?' He chuckled.

'It was the perfect blend of tacky and ridiculousness. I can't believe you went to so much trouble just for me.'

'You're worth it.' He shook his head again.

'I still can't believe you're here. You're actually *here*. When did you fly in?'

Pierce checked his watch. 'About three hours ago. I had the idea for the video and Molly helped make it happen. We knew you'd be out on house calls this morning, so it seemed the perfect opportunity to do all the photography then.'

'But I still don't know how it was edited together so fast and—' She held up her hand. 'You know what? I don't want to know.' She pressed a kiss to Pierce's lips. 'I just want to enjoy.'

It was a lot of kisses later when Stacey looked deeply into his eyes and said softly, 'You once told me you could see loneliness in my eyes, my sad eyes, and it was true. It was there because something was missing from my life— something just for me, something precious and rare. And that's you. You were what was missing from my life.'

'Marry me soon, Stacey,' he remarked as he kissed her yet again, unable to get enough of her delectable mouth.

'Of course. And that, my love, will be a definite dream come true.'

EPILOGUE

THE WEDDING WAS held outside in Nell's backyard a few weeks after New Year. Pierce had
waited only the least amount of time it took
to have their banns read before he married the
woman of his dreams.

'Do you remember how we used to pretend
that we'd get married in this very back garden?'
Cora asked as she made the final touches to Stacey's hairstyle before putting a garland of flowers carefully in place. 'Oh!' She gasped. 'You
look just like we always imagined. Like a prin-
cess at a small backyard wedding with our closest family and friends and we have Mike ready
to walk you down the garden aisle, giving you
away.'

Molly clutched her hands to her chest before
tying Lydia's sash, which had come undone
again. All of Stacey's sisters, including Nell,
were with her, getting ready. George was with

Pierce in the room down the hall. The wedding celebrant was an old family friend of her parents and the garden was filled with their closest friends.

'Nervous?' Jasmine asked, and Stacey wrinkled her nose.

'No. Not even worried. I get to marry Pierce today. My handsome prince. This time it's the real deal.'

Molly took one of her hands and Cora took the other, all the triplets standing together, grinning at each other, sharing incredible emotions.

'This is right, Stace. He's so perfect for you.'

'And you're so perfect for him.'

'Thank you.' Stacey looked to the two women who had been with her for ever. They were sisters, and sisters were never wrong.

Jasmine rallied Lydia and Nell into position as Edna came in to check everyone was ready.

'Pierce is impatiently awaiting your arrival,' Edna told them as Mike came to offer Stacey his arm.

Both Edna and Mike looked at her.

'Oh, your father would have been right proud to see this day,' Mike told her.

'So proud,' Edna agreed, and kissed Stacey on the cheek. '*We're* so proud—aren't we, Mike?'

'Yes. We're proud of all of you.' Mike's gaze encompassed them all. 'And of little George, of course,' he added, which made Lydia giggle, and the sound of Lydia's giggle made the rest of them giggle too.

It was just the tension release they all needed, so that when the music started Stacey proudly took her place at the bottom of the garden.

Her smile only increased when she saw Pierce standing there, waiting expectantly for her. She floated towards him, not caring whether she walked in time to the music, not caring if anything went wrong. Pierce was looking at her as though she were the most stunning woman in the world, and she knew in her heart that was exactly what he thought because he'd told her so—quite often.

'You look...*wow*!' They were the first words out of his mouth as she came to stand beside him, her simple white sundress and flat white shoes enhanced by the wild flowers in her hair and bouquet. *Au naturel*. No fuss. No big puffy dress. Not this time. *This* was her dream wedding. Simple. Casual. Family.

'You look pretty wow yourself,' she told him as she took in his light grey suit.

'Ready to get married?'

'To you? Absolutely.'

She reached for his hand, linking her fingers with his, unable to believe such a pure, perfect happiness as this existed, and that it was a happiness that, for them, would last for ever.

* * * * *

MILLS & BOON®
Large Print Medical

April

IT STARTED WITH NO STRINGS…	Kate Hardy
ONE MORE NIGHT WITH HER DESERT PRINCE…	Jennifer Taylor
FLIRTING WITH DR OFF-LIMITS	Robin Gianna
FROM FLING TO FOREVER	Avril Tremayne
DARE SHE DATE AGAIN?	Amy Ruttan
THE SURGEON'S CHRISTMAS WISH	Annie O'Neil

May

PLAYING THE PLAYBOY'S SWEETHEART	Carol Marinelli
UNWRAPPING HER ITALIAN DOC	Carol Marinelli
A DOCTOR BY DAY…	Emily Forbes
TAMED BY THE RENEGADE	Emily Forbes
A LITTLE CHRISTMAS MAGIC	Alison Roberts
CHRISTMAS WITH THE MAVERICK MILLIONAIRE	Scarlet Wilson

June

MIDWIFE'S CHRISTMAS PROPOSAL	Fiona McArthur
MIDWIFE'S MISTLETOE BABY	Fiona McArthur
A BABY ON HER CHRISTMAS LIST	Louisa George
A FAMILY THIS CHRISTMAS	Sue MacKay
FALLING FOR DR DECEMBER	Susanne Hampton
SNOWBOUND WITH THE SURGEON	Annie Claydon

MILLS & BOON®
Large Print Medical

July

HOW TO FIND A MAN IN FIVE DATES	Tina Beckett
BREAKING HER NO-DATING RULE	Amalie Berlin
IT HAPPENED ONE NIGHT SHIFT	Amy Andrews
TAMED BY HER ARMY DOC'S TOUCH	Lucy Ryder
A CHILD TO BIND THEM	Lucy Clark
THE BABY THAT CHANGED HER LIFE	Louisa Heaton

August

A DATE WITH HER VALENTINE DOC	Melanie Milburne
IT HAPPENED IN PARIS...	Robin Gianna
THE SHEIKH DOCTOR'S BRIDE	Meredith Webber
TEMPTATION IN PARADISE	Joanna Neil
A BABY TO HEAL THEIR HEARTS	Kate Hardy
THE SURGEON'S BABY SECRET	Amber McKenzie

September

BABY TWINS TO BIND THEM	Carol Marinelli
THE FIREFIGHTER TO HEAL HER HEART	Annie O'Neil
TORTURED BY HER TOUCH	Dianne Drake
IT HAPPENED IN VEGAS	Amy Ruttan
THE FAMILY SHE NEEDS	Sue MacKay
A FATHER FOR POPPY	Abigail Gordon

0315 LP 2P P2 M